MEEHALL

A Time Travel Romance

JANE STAIN

A QUICK NOTE ABOUT THE HISTORICAL SETTING FOR MEEHALL

The Scots are feisty and fiercely independent. Have you ever wondered how England got Scotland under its power? The story of Scotland's surrender to England went something like this:

The Scots Parliament saw England and Spain colonizing the world and bringing home treasures unimaged. They wanted in on that action.

Despite the disapproval of their king, they scoured the globe, searching for the best place to put a Scottish colony. One that would bring them wealth. One that was different from all the other colonies.

They settled on The Darien Bay of faraway Panama. They would have their colonists dig a canal through the isthmus. Scotland's leaders would get rich charging England and Spain's ships for passage!

So in the 1690s, more than two hundred years before the Panama Canal was finished, Scotland started it. The Scottish leaders committed their kingdom's wealth and almost three thousand settlers to founding a Scottish colony.

They named this colony Caledonia, the name the Romans had used for Scotland.

Scotland's leaders failed, however, to anticipate Spain's military response. Furious at the invasion into their declared territory, Spain blockaded Darien Bay and lay siege to Caledonia, whose settlers were already plagued by disease.

The Scots called on their allies for help. The indigenous people of Panama, called the Kuna today, came to the aid of the Scots, but they were no match for the Spanish Empire. England blockaded their other allies from sailing to their aid.

Abandoning the colony in March of 1700 to the Kuna —who still live there and call it Caledonia— left Scotland in financial ruin. Only half of the settlers made it home.

England 'came to the rescue' and proposed an Act of Union.

Scotland accepted, and in 1707, Scotland and England became a new nation called Great Britain.

Most of the following story takes place in Scotland in 1706 amid the common people's anger at their leaders' reckless loss of life and wealth, not to mention rumors of a pending union with England.

The Darien Chest held the money and documents of the Company of Scotland. Now on display in the National Museum of Scotland in Edinburgh, it has a beautiful mechanical locking mechanism. Photo taken by Kim Traynor - Own work, CC BY-SA 3.0 https://commons.wikimedia.org/w/index.php?curid=15854408

When Sarah first started her job here at Celtic University, it had seemed glamorous. All those years she re-enacted Scottish history as a teen, she had only dreamed of one day translating ancient Gaelic texts and inscriptions. A year later, it just amounted to typing all day. And sweeping up the piles of dust these ancient texts and artifacts left on the floor.

Checking to make sure no one could see her and then twirling the broom around her like a quarter-staff on her way to put it up, she looked out through the bevel leaded-glass recently added to the ancient arrow-slit window in the wall made of gray stones the size of her head.

The Highlands lurked out there in all their Scottish glory: lush thistled meadows between soaring gray-stone mountains backed by stormy clouds with brooding personality.

Wrinkling her nose in embarrassment, she recalled how excited she'd been when she first got here, thrilled just be able to have this view all the time. Now, she longed to be out there having her own adventures, rather than sitting here inside, typing about the adventures of others. These ancient Celtic myths and legends were full of Druid magic, tests of wit, Scottish castles, and forbidden love. Who wouldn't want to take part?

A pang of guilt took her, remembering the fit her old friend had thrown when Sarah admitted she was thinking of quitting the job Kelsey had pulled strings to get her. But If Sarah no longer liked her job, then she ought to be able to quit without her friends complaining about it, right?

After all, Kelsey didn't owe Celtic University half the loyalty she showed. They had made Kelsey a Druid without her knowledge or consent. Well, okay, being a Druid was kind of cool, but to do something like that against someone's will was unforgivable.

Kelsey's undying loyalty to Celtic U was downright foolish.

With a deep sigh, Sarah turned away from her fantasies outside and considered the pile of ancient Celtic artifacts on her desk, looking for the next one she would work on. It didn't really matter. They had all blended into one boring lump of 'same old, same old.'

However, the choice was taken away from her. Gertrude, Chief Secretary at the University, came over to Sarah's desk. "This has just come to us from on high. It is to be the very next thing you work on. And be quick about it. They want it as soon as possible." With that, Sarah's boss unceremoniously plopped an object down under Sarah's nose before walking back toward her office at the end of the room full of desks like Sarah's.

But Sarah wasn't concerned with anything her boss had said. No, her heart was racing and she was trying her hardest not to hyperventilate.

Because the iron bracer on her desk was familiar. She'd seen it in a dream Kelsey had shared with her, a dream compiled of the memories of a mutual friend who had once been much more than a friend, years ago back at the Renaissance Faire.

Kelsey could do that. Dream walking was her magical druidic specialty. She was able to enter the dreams —and thus conjure the memories— of anyone she'd ever touched, and back in their teens, the 12 of them had been inseparable:

Sarah and Michael (Meehall in Gaelic), Ashley and Gabriel (Meehall's twin, who took the Gaelic name Conall once he was 13, because Gabriel was considered weak and feminine);

Lauren and Jeff (Meehall's younger brother), Jaelle and John (Eoin, Jeff's twin, the 4th son of Dall's first son, Peadar);

Kelsey and Tavish (Meehall's uncle of the same age), Amber and Tomas (Tavish's older twin).

Yes, it was weird there were three sets of twins, but that wasn't the half of it. All the guys had disappeared from all the girls' lives the day before the oldest set of twins, Tavish and Tomas, turned 18. Kelsey and Amber were back together with Tavish and Tomas now, but the rest of them were still parted. Oh, Kelsey had explained the guys were just trying to save their girlfriends from the family curse, but Meehall's desertion still stung.

Anyway, the bracer on Sarah's desk brought to mind the most recent memories of Meehall's that Kelsey had shared with Sarah, in all their heartbreaking details.

Looking gorgeous in his kilt, Meehall played with his sons. They were five, four, and three years old, and they lived with him among the Murray clan in 1706. Meehall's father was from the 1500s, and Meehall had distant cousins among the Murray clan.

Meehall and his family were really MacGregors, but that name had been outlawed, and so the Murrays had taken them in. The clan slogan, 'MacGregor despite them,' so strong in the new world, lived on here in Scotland only in telling the children they were really MacGregors.

The game he played with his sons resembled hockey, but with natural sticks and a ball made of knotted cloth. The children ran after and around their father, all three ganging up on him, trying to get the ball away, enthusiastically coaching each other in Gaelic.

"'Tis ower there!"

"I hae this side!"

"He is gaun'ae run!"

"We hae tae stay with him!"

The sounds of their laughter hit Sarah's heart with mixed feelings. On the one hand, the little Scots were adorable; who wouldn't love them? On the other hand, they were his with another woman.

Jealousy was petty, especially now, nine years after Meehall left her. But try as she might, Sarah couldn't shake off the green-eyed monster.

Meehall's memories shifted back to the time when his wife, Cairstine, was alive. Blonde and beautiful, she'd been the vision of a Celtic goddess. Statuesque, while mousey-haired Sarah was more the girl next door.

Seeing Meehall with Cairstine made Sarah's heart hurt in a way she couldn't bear. But she knew the woman had died, and so instead of anger, her heart went out to Meehall. Losing his children's mother must've devastated him.

Meehall's memories moved forward in the dream. He was happy, hunting with his distant cousins. Ciaran and Baltaire both had dark hair and eyes like Meehall's parents, while Meehall himself had strawberry blond hair and blue eyes. His grandfather, Dall, said Meehall and Conall were the spit and image of their great grandmother. She lived in the 1500s, so they had to take Dall's word for it.

Meehall's memories drifted to when Cairstine took sick. He had to take her to a safe location, because wherever he was when he left this time period, that's where he would return, and there was a dangerous feud on, between the Murrays and the Camerons.

Meehall carried his wife to a cave, went inside, and put on the bracer. It was cumbersome, not something he wore all the time.

The world swirled around them, blurring as if they had fallen off a galloping horse and were spinning through the air on their way to the ground.

Meehall and Cairstine materialized inside old Chancellor Stanley's office, here at Celtic University.

Sarah knew the room, because all the secretaries were frequently called into it whenever the old man wanted to give them what he called praise, but what they grumbled about as tedium, when he wasn't around.

Stanley's office was large. The man's huge desk only took up one corner, and there were couches and armchairs enough for two dozen secretaries to sit in, as well as a fireplace, a reading table, and a dozen bookcases.

Meehall and his sick wife had arrived in this room during Meehall's real timeline here in the 21st century—

Which Sarah now realized had been just a few weeks before Kelsey got her this job. Why hadn't she realized that before? Wait. Wait just a darn second. She had realized it before. Why had she forgotten? It seemed significant.

The old Chancellor came into his office just as Meehall and Cairstine arrived. "'Tis sorry I am, Meehall, but I canna allow ye to take her outside o' this room. The exposure would be too great. She does na have the training to go into the modern waurld—"

Meehall drew his sword, rushing the old man.

But Stanley merely held up his hand.

Frozen in place, Meehall seethed, "Then get a doctor tae come here. If ye dinna, her blood will be on yer hands."

The Chancellor gave Meehall a sad smile. "Nay, I canna do that either. This modern time has too many ways the secret o' time travel would be revealed if I did so. Nay, she is gaun'ae have to die, and that is too bad. Ye only have three sons."

The world spun again. Meehall and Cairstine were back in the 1700s.

And then time had flown forward and Meehall was alone, crying.

Meehall's memories let her know the bracer always brought him to that room and that when he wanted to go back to the past, he always had to leave from that room.

Sarah also remembered now that Meehall resented this stipulation by the Druids who ran Celtic University. Why hadn't she remembered that before? No wonder Kelsey walked on eggshells around the other druids, if they meddled this much in people's lives. And no wonder Meehall kept showing up at Celtic. Why hadn't Kelsey just reminded her of that when Sarah complained about him being here? Because complain, she had.

Sarah tried to keep her own memories of Meehall from taking over, but they were relentless. Circle dances out on the field away from the rest of the faire in the evenings when the breeze was cool and the sun no longer beat down on them. Sarah learning the quarterstaff next to Meehall learning the sword. Sneaking away from faire business-meetings together in order to make out in the spice booth, whose owner always took the spices home for the night, not wanting them to get damp if it rained. Sharing a tent with all the other girlfriends that first summer —until her parents figured out the girls were all dating brothers and probably shouldn't be left alone at night.

Tears came to Sarah's eyes, thinking about how close she'd been with Meehall. She had thought it would never end, right up to that day nine years ago, when all six of the guys simply disappeared.

🐚

FORTUNATELY, IT WAS TIME FOR LUNCH. SARAH had a good excuse to put off describing the inscriptions on the bracer in such a way that even foreign professors would understand them. The druids went to a lot of trouble to fit in with the academic community so as not to raise suspicions, which meant keeping an extensive intranet, open only to their colleagues at other universities.

But Sarah didn't have a good excuse for slipping the bracer into her bag.

She knew she should have their mutual friend Kelsey give it back to Meehall, in the course of which Kelsey could explain to Gertrude the bracer wasn't something they should keep in the office. That would've been the sensible thing to do.

However, even though Sarah perfectly understood Meehall had left her to protect her from his family's curse, she wanted to make him suffer for leaving her. Just for a little while.

Walking the old stone hallways decorated with ancient runes had been bliss when Sarah first arrived here at Celtic. Now, even as she admired its beauty, she cursed every time she tripped over the uneven stone flooring, and she groaned when she entered the formal dining room with its high ceilings that made everything echo. She wanted to be out there enjoying the Highlands, not cooped up in this stuffy old school. Who knew you could get cabin fever in a place this large?

Nadia and Ellie were already seated at their usual table in the corner.

"Did someone eat your lunch?" Nadia teased. "I've never seen you this upset." Her gray eyes softened a bit, and she brushed her long brown hair back behind her olive-skinned shoulder in order to lean over and give Sarah a sideways hug. "I was hoping you would help me soften Gertrude up for my transfer to the ballads department, but what's the matter?"

Ellie's usually joyful freckled face bunched up in concern, and her red curly hair jiggled as she leaned over quickly to hug Sarah from the other side. "Yeah, what's wrong? Need us to go beat someone up for you?"

Despite herself, Sarah chuckled at Ellie's joke,

hugging her friends in return. "I almost didn't come to lunch, but then I remembered you would cheer me up. No, there's no one to beat up this time."

They all laughed at the idea of Ellie and Nadia beating anyone up. Sarah's friends were strong enough, Ellie being a hiker and Nadia a dancer, but there wasn't a mean bone in their bodies. It was almost as if Gertrude looked for meekness when she hired clerks. That was why Sarah only practiced her quarterstaff moves in the privacy of her dorm room, or on the sly with her broom.

Ellie pointedly turned back toward the bank of a hundred tiny leaded glass windows. "Well as it happens, Nadia and I were just discussing something that will cheer you up." She leaned in toward Sarah, pulling Nadia in with her before she whispered, "We're calling in sick tomorrow to go to the carnival that's come to town. Call in sick too, and come with us."

Sarah guffawed, then whispered back, "Yeah, because that wouldn't be at all suspicious: all three American clerks calling in sick on the same day after sitting here with our heads together."

Her friends looked repentant and started to sit back, away from her.

But Sarah hugged them to her again. "You don't

have any need to call in sick tomorrow. I just thought of a way to get back at the person who made me so mad just now. I'm taking the two of you back in time."

Both of her friends burst out laughing.

"Good one!" Ellie said with a thumbs up and a freckle-faced wink. "I'll make a jokester out of you yet!"

"You know we would both love to go back in time," Nadia scolded with that wise look she could summon into her gray eyes when she sang. "Don't tease us."

Sarah smiled at them like the cat who ate the canary, then spoke in a low whisper while smiling nonchalantly in case anyone from another table was watching them because they had laughed so loudly. "I'm not teasing. Consider where we work, and with what." She wiped her mouth, carefully folded her napkin so as to attract her friends' attention, and then gently laid it on her empty plate.

It worked. Both of them were staring at her.

She smiled at them in the way of someone holding back a surprise, then patted the bulge the bracer was making in her bag, under the table. "Don't take your afternoon break. Take off work fifteen minutes early instead and meet me here. I need to show you something."

"I don't know," Ellie teased, "that's when I usually go on my run. I really shouldn't miss it, not even for one day when you show us something awesome."

They didn't waste any time jumping up and gathering their things from the next table, anxious to get back early so they could get the day's work done and leave a little early.

"This is a nice turn of events."

"Yeah, she always knows just what we need to do in order for a plan to work, and she goes from 'down in the dumps' to 'Let's go have some fun' really quick. She's always full of ideas. That's what I love about Sarah."

❧

After work, Sarah rushed them out of the dining hall and down the dirt path.

Her friends followed on her heels, speculating.

"We going to the chemistry lab?"

"Nope. The gym?"

"Wouldn't that be funny, watching Sarah fall over herself trying to do gymnastics?"

They both laughed, looking forward to their surprise. Good.

"Oh, the theatre!"

Sarah knocked on the back door.

When Janice opened it, she gave Sarah a grateful look and gestured them in. "You caught me just as I was leaving," she said in her English accent. "What a nice surprise."

"You think so?" Sarah was looking over Janice's shoulder at the stairs to the basement, where all the costumes were kept. "I was hoping you'd let us borrow some of the wardrobe from last year's production of Macbeth."

Janice raised her eyebrows. "You are aware you will need to tell me what for?"

This was the part Sarah wasn't looking forward to. She hated lying. But there was no way she was going to tell Janice the truth. They would have to take her with them, along with anyone she told. Where would it end? "We're making a video."

Janice looked toward Nadia and Ellie.

Ellie wrinkled her cute freckled nose and shrugged adorably.

Nadia shrugged just one shoulder in that off-hand way she had.

Janice turned back to Sarah with a frank smile

that said she wasn't keen on staying half an hour late at work to help them find costumes that fit, but she owed Sarah a favor in exchange for advice on how to deal with her hovering mother. Out loud, all Janice said was "I guess so. Here, I'll show you where they are."

Sarah followed Janice down the narrow stone staircase into the coolness of the dark basement beneath the theater. "I'm pleasantly surprised. I was worried it would be musty down here."

Janice flipped on the electric lights. "Nah, we have a sump pump and dehumidifier. Here's where we keep the costumes for 'The Scottish play.' Which parts do you want?"

Nadia headed toward Lady Macbeth's black velvet with elation on her face.

With a bit of regret because black velvet would flatter Nadia's gray eyes, Sarah grabbed her friend by the shirt. "Just the background players, the farm folk in plaid."

After twenty minutes of fuss, olive-skinned and brown-haired Nadia looked absolutely stunning in a brown leine with a gray plaid pattern that matched her eyes, paired with a brown and light blue plaid wrap for her shoulders. "Why do we have to wear the costumes on our way back to the dorm?"

"We're only going to the dorm to get some stuff," Sarah told her out of the corner of her mouth while rushing the two of them along the path, "and then we have to go to the offices." This was the only place they could ask questions, being far away from everybody, so she wanted to encourage them to ask as many as possible now. She knew the best way to do that was to seem to be discouraging questions. Those college psychology classes Sarah had taken instead of hard science were paying off.

With her freckles, Ellie was always cute, but the green plaid she had chosen set off her curly red hair, and the rust-colored leine matched her freckles in a pleasing way. "What could we possibly need to go the offices for?"

Sarah gave her friend a significant look. "Stanley is hiding more than dusty old books in that huge room of his. One of us wears this," she tapped the lump in her backpack, "while touching the others on a spot in Stanley's office, and off we go."

Her friends' excitement was palpable, and once they were in her dorm room, Sarah smiled to herself while she grabbed whatever she thought she might need and shoved it in a leather backpack Kelsey had given her —a nice survival one that had all sorts of hidden gizmos built in, yet looked like a simple leather pack.

"All right" she said to their eager faces. "For this first trip into the past, we're just going to look around old Inverness a few hours, where it's safe and comfortable. So I've packed everything I can think of we might need, including a first aid kit and some period coins Kelsey gave me." She showed them the colorful assortment of coins in different metals, some copper, but many silver.

Nadia turned a wise eye on Sarah. "I bet that money goes much farther than you might think. You're so lucky Kelsey's your friend. I think you better offer one of those coins at a time when paying for things, and start with the copper ones."

Ellie was already out the door and down the hall, and sharing amused grins, Sarah and Nadia rushed after her, into her room.

"I have the perfect boots to wear with this outfit!" Ellie gushed while changing into them from her sneakers. "What do you think?"

"They are perfect," Nadia admired. Caressing their soft leather, her face turned soft and thoughtful. "I just might have something that will work for me, too."

They visited Nadia's room as well, but neither of

them had a suitable bag, so Sarah put the things they thought they would need in hers.

It was time to do this. "Come on." She turned back to them and lowered her voice to the barest whisper. "We're going to Stanley's office."

2

Meehall jumped out of the small bed in a panic. What was he doing in the modern world?

Needing to relieve himself, he got up and looked around —and remembered. He was in a dorm room at Celtic University, headquarters of the modern Druids. One of his oldest friends had surprised him with a summons here for a meeting yesterday. An unsettling meeting.

❧

MEEHALL KNOCKED ON THE ANCIENT WOODEN door across the graystone hallway from Meehall's time travel locus in Chancellor Stanley's office.

When his friend Kelsey opened it, she studied him. "The 1700s agree with you. I've never seen you healthier." She held out her arms for a hug.

Meehall hugged her, then closed the door behind him. "Thank you. I could say the same for you about the 1300s."

She stood relaxed and sociable, raising her hand to indicate a nice catered lunch on the table in the corner. "Please, join me."

Kelsey's gesture made the blood drain from Meehall's face. On the surface, it was simply polite. But he had seen that exact same gesture before. Made by the Druids. More exactly, the strain of Druids who had enslaved his family five hundred years ago, forcing the MacGregors to do time travel errands for them. They ran Celtic University, and Kelsey was one of their star graduates.

A second later, when his subconscious had processed all this, the battle heat rose up in him, tightening his muscles, making him itch to draw a sword he didn't currently have.

Because of his grandfather Dall's amended arrangement with the Druids who ran Celtic, Meehall could live in the past. His three sons had a whole clan to help raise them. He hunted with his cousins, helped in the feud with the Camerons, and was a genuine Highlander. A dream come true.

Meehall was grateful. He was. But at times he thought the price his family paid for time travel was too high.

Keeping his face carefully neutral, he only said, "So why did ye send for me?"

Kelsey laughed, and for a moment it lit up her face like it had back at the Renaissance faire, where his same-age uncle Tavish fell in love with her when they were all teens.

Meehall had fallen in love with Sarah at the faire, too. And now that Cairstine was gone, thoughts of Sarah filled his mind often. How was she?

Kelsey was still smiling at him. "No reason, really. I just wanted to see you. I'm your aunt now, you know, through marriage. Can't a person miss her nephew?"

Something was up. Kelsey's normal worksite was the dig at Dunskey Castle, hours away from here. But she obviously wasn't going to tell him what was going on, and the chance of her letting something slip would decrease immensely if he asked her.

So Meehall just smiled back. "Of course a person can miss her nephew who's just a year younger. It's nice to see you. I trust Tavish is well?"

She gestured at the food. "Please, let's eat." She herself picked up a sandwich and took a bite, giving him her 'isn't this delicious' face.

Meehall dug in, and oh, it was good. He hadn't had white bread in years, let alone Red Bull. "I see you remember what I like." He did give her a friendly smile after that observation. It had been nice of her.

She gave him an oddly knowing look for a moment, but then her face dissolved into the friendliness she'd been sporting since he arrived. "Aye, Tavish is very happy, both in modern times and in the 1300s. We both are." She gently placed her hand on his. "But how are you, Meehall? I'm so sorry for your loss."

He had been fine until she brought it up. Cairstine's death never truly left him. After a year, it had softened a bit, but it was always there in the back of his mind, ready to crush him in sorrow whenever something reminded him of her. His sons were a constant reminder, and he had to admit he spent more and more time away from them, leaving them in the loving care of their clan.

But he didn't want to tell Kelsey all that, so he just said, "It's getting better, the grief."

It had been an okay meeting, but he still didn't understand why she had called it. They had simply shared a meal and exchanged pleasantries. Truth to tell, seeing Kelsey so Druid-like had ruined his fond memories of her.

Well, he would just go home. Ciaran and Baltair were waiting for him to get back before they went on their next hunting trip. Alan was about to lose his first tooth, and his brothers Keith and Lyle were all excited about the prospect of holding a human tooth in their hands. Aye, he should have gone home last night. Why had he slept here, again?

Well, that was strange. He could have sworn he left his bracer right here on the nightstand. Had he left it in his bag? No, it wasn't in there. He pulled the bedclothes off the bed and shook them, but no sign of it. With a sinking feeling, he got down on all fours and looked under the bed. Nope. Opened all the drawers of the dresser. No. And the desk. No.

Had he been so surprised at the change in Kelsey that he left it in her office? That had to be it. He only thought about showering for a split second before he dismissed the idea, kilted himself, and went back to the office building to knock on her door.

But it wasn't Kelsey who answered. No, it was Gertrude, Chancellor Stanley's secretary. "Hello,

Meehall. Is there some aught I can help ye with afore yer meeting with the Chancellor in a few minutes?"

"I wasna aware I was meeting with the Chancellor."

"Aye, he's verra anxious tae see ye."

"Afore I go ower there, I'd like tae hae a word with Kelsey, if ye dinna mind."

"O' course I dinna mind, but she isna here."

"I may hae left someaught in here yesterday when I was meeting with her. May I come in and hae a look?"

With an odd look he didn't quite understand, she gestured him in, then watched him look around.

Hopeful, he looked first on the floor near where he had sat at the luncheon table. No. Puzzled, he looked on the bookshelf nearby. No. Fighting panic, he looked on the floor around the table, and then went down on the floor to look under the desk.

No sign of it. The bracer was gone.

And the Chancellor wanted to see him. This couldn't be a coincidence.

Meehall nodded politely at Gertrude as he left Kelsey's office and turned to knock on the door across the hall.

"Come in, come in," Chancellor Stanley called from inside. Upon seeing Meehall enter, his face brightened in a frightening imitation of friendliness. From behind his massive desk, he gestured to where a computer had been set up on his reading table in the center of the room. "We need ye tae complete some tests regarding the influence o' time travel on ye. 'Twill take up the better part o' yer day, I fear, and then we hae a banquet tae attend, but after that ye wull be free tae gae..."

Meehall fully intended to fly through the computerized tests with nary a care for accuracy, but quite against his will, he found them fascinating. They asked about his personal life more than he was comfortable with, but he knew full well the druids could delve into his memories magically. So he answered truthfully. They were undoubtedly holding onto his bracer until after he finished. May as well get it over with.

As he rode to the banquet with Meehall in the back of his limousine, the Chancellor only said a few words. "I ken I dinna need tae tell ye this, but o' course ye make nary a mention o' time travel. The University's story is that ye are involved in oor immersive 'living history' study o' the area aroond Inverness in 1706, working as a reenactor at historical sites."

There was always a story. It was important for

Celtic to seem like a normal research institution that made its money by taking in students, like other universities around the world.

"I understand," was all Meehall said. He had long ago given up trying to convince them to change their ways. What would be the point? All that did was make them keep him longer, here in the present.

The longer Meehall was away from his new life, the more anxious he grew. Sure, the boys were safe with his clan, but he didn't want to leave them there without him for good. And the longer he was detained by the powers at Celtic, the more he started to suspect that was the plan. He was like a Guinea pig to them, and apparently so were his children.

As usual, the Chancellor's office hadn't allowed Meehall to leave with his sword, not into modern times. The excuse was he needn't alarm the students, but he knew full well the Druids didn't want him armed in their presence. He still had his bare hands though, and perhaps these modern Druids didn't realize just what lethal weapons those were. He wasn't some lab rat to be manipulated with the promise of cheese.

He spent a boring afternoon lying to the professors at other universities about how interesting it was to reenact the period he really lived in, and then the limousine took them back to Celtic and stopped in front of the office building.

The Chancellor walked up the steps. "Ye can use that dorm room as long as ye like."

Meehall rushed ahead and pushed the door open with more force than necessary. "I wull gae home now, sae give me my bracer."

Oh no.

Meehall broke into a run down the long hallway toward the Chancellor's door. Knowing he wouldn't reach it in time, he strained his legs and ran with all he had, pushing himself to the point of pain with every stride.

Because Sarah was unlocking the Chancellor's office. She had two friends with her. They were all wearing period clothing. And on her right forearm was his bracer.

3

Sarah rushed her friends into Stanley's office as fast as she could, all but dragging them over to the spot on the floor where they needed to be in order to time travel. The bracer was already on her, so they should go as soon as they got there. She held tight to their hands, making sure they went with her, and huddled them all into the spot.

At first, they held her hands tightly, with excitement. But gradually, their grips loosened, until they were looking at her with betrayal and disappointment in their eyes.

Sarah's heart sank. Why wasn't the bracer taking them back in time, already? Meehall's memories just said he had to be wearing it in this spot. "Maybe I need to take the bracer off and put it back on again, to reset it."

Serene gray-eyed Nadia gave her a tentative smile of encouragement. "Yeah, maybe."

But the jaded bitterness red-haired Ellie tried to hide with all her jokes came out. "Come on. This was a good joke you played on us, Sarah. Very elaborate. But it's played out. Don't belabor it beyond when its funny. Ha ha."

Sarah subtly and gently pushed her friends against the desk in order to lean on them and maintain the needed contact while freeing her hands so she could take the bracer off and put it back on again. Getting it on over the billowing sleeves of her period peasant costume was tricky, but at last she managed.

The old leather-bound books on the wooden shelves blurred and spun as if they were underwater on the sides of a pool that was draining. Nausea came up, but Sarah grabbed her friends and held on, lest she be alone on this adventure.

Thankfully, the whirling stopped after just a few moments. She didn't think she could take anymore. Meehall's memories hadn't contained any of the nausea she felt. Hopefully this would be worth it—

Ellie and Nadia were now squeezing her hands so hard, she was brought out of her thoughts quickly.

And thank goodness, because they were no longer at the university, but rather in a tiny upstairs room. An inn room, from the looks of it.

"Good," she told Nadia and Ellie, "Meehall must hae rented a room for the time he would be in the 21st Century, which means we hae a place tae retreat tae, should it get tae much oot there."

Sarah promptly dragged the two over to the glassless window. Pulling up the curtain so they could see out into the street, she asked them the loaded question. "Look oot, then, and tell me what ye think."

Ellie's tone changed to one of amazement. "Would ye look at that?"

Nadia chimed in. "Aye! I hae tae hand it tae ye, Sarah. It does look like we hae gone back in time."

Sarah let them stare out the window a minute. Truth to tell, she was enjoying the sights as well. People walked or rode, either in carriages or on horseback. The clop of hooves rang out on the cobblestones, and shopkeepers hawked their wares to passersby.

"Hats, hats! Ye could dae with a fine new hat."

"Shoes! Master cobbler-made shoes. Repairs as wull."

Inverness wasn't as big now as it had been in

their time, of course. If Sarah craned her neck and looked down the street, she could see the city wall on either side. But still, it was a sizable place.

The people walking about wore clothes much more sophisticated than Sarah, Nadia, and Ellie's outfits. The men wore actual suit coats and short trousers, and the women wore long one-piece dresses that buttoned up the back. Those who walked carried shopping baskets, and everyone wore hats and gloves. Some had on long overcoats.

Apparently, Nadia had noticed this too. "Oh, if only we could gae doon there and buy some o' those clothes. Wouldna we be the envy o' everyone at work tomorrow?"

"Aye," Ellie gushed, "We would."

Sarah finally let go of their hands, confident they wouldn't run off into the unknown without the appropriate caution. "It just sae happens we can, but we must stay together, ye ken?"

Both women gave Sarah quizzical looks, but they followed her to the door —and gasped when she opened it. The closed door and their proximity to the window had kept the sounds and scents of the downstairs tavern away, but now the aroma of freshly baked bannocks and lamb stew wafted up.

"Let us gae doon and hae some," said Nadia, practically dancing to the door.

Sarah rushed ahead of her friends and made it to the stairs first, looking back over her shoulder at them with as stern a look as she could manage, considering her own excitement. "Aye, let us. But we stay together. And nay talk o' home. These people will na understand, remember."

Nadia nodded sagely, her body moving to the lilting music of a fiddle that had started to play a lively tune down there in the tavern.

Ellie rolled her eyes and threw her hands up in the air, grinning at Nadia with mock amusement which was really impatience, knowing her. "Just humor her." She turned to Sarah. "Verra wull, we will na tell anyone here about home. Are ye happy?"

But Sarah stared her friends down. "Ye will na give us away as time travelers, and ye will stay with me."

Nadia chuckled, and like all the sounds she made, it was musical. "Aye, we will stay with ye."

"Good, keep speaking Gaelic. No telling what would happen if we spoke tae these people in modern English."

Her friends looked surprised at the realization

they had been speaking Gaelic, but they eagerly agreed.

Finally satisfied, Sarah turned around and led them down into the tavern.

Their gasps of surprise satisfied her immensely.

Surveying the bustling room, Ellie whispered, "I canna believe it. We really hae gone back in time. I thought ye were having us on, had drugged us and dragged us tae auld Inverness or some aught. But nay. There is na other explanation. Look how much smoke is in the room, from the fireplace and all the lamps. And the lasses are all sae demure, even that one ower there, the slattern. All that talk o' lasses's liberation in school just seemed ridiculous till now, when I see the reality o' just how bad 'twas. Every last one o' these lasses is looking tae a man for protection—"

Sarah turned and shushed her friend just as they got to the bottom of the staircase, then looked up to make sure Nadia wasn't going to blurt out any of the same thoughts.

But Nadia was pale and compliant —for the first time Sarah could remember.

Assured that no one had heard them over the hubbub in the tavern, Sarah cupped her hand under the small period purse attached to her belt to keep the period coins Kelsey had given her from jingling.

Out of habit, they sat at a corner table.

Meeting Nadia's eyes to acknowledge her wisdom, Sarah discreetly put the purse inside her leather satchel under the table. then carefully took out just a few coins, which she stowed in her bosom. Once they entered the tavern, the little period purse dangling from her belt had looked like a ridiculously easy thing to steal. They didn't call thieves cutpurses for nothing.

A serving wench came over. "One copper each for the meal. Half if ye just want ale." How old must she be? Her face looked like she was 40, but there wasn't any gray in her hair.

Nadia and Ellie both blanched, but they looked impressed when Sarah dug three coppers out of her bosom and handed them over with a smile.

The three of them sat waiting for their food in silence, but their eyes and faces said to each other, "How amazing is this! We've gone back in time!" "I know! Just look at all these people, the clothes they're wearing and the way they talk."

The tavern talk was interesting.

"We canna let the English win, and our admitting their alien act has cost us money we canna dae withoot would be England winning."

"What is Scotland tae live on, then?"

"I dinna ken."

"If ye ask me, 'tis all the fault o' those lowlanders and their accursed Darien Scheme."

The food came, and it tasted just as good as it smelled, fresh ingredients and home cooking would do that. But before they were even finished eating, they were all anxiously looking out the door whenever someone came or went.

The sun hung in the sky at about 3 o'clock on a brisk March day.

Stretching her arms toward the ceiling so that the huge sleeves of her MacBeth costume fell down around her long brown hair, Nadia said what they were all thinking. "If we are gaun'ae explore the toon, we must needs gae now. There is but a few hours o' daylight left."

"Aye," Ellie said, jumping up.

Smiling with anticipation, Sarah jumped up as well. "Nadia, lead the way."

With a dramatic dancer's swirl of her long skirts, Nadia got up.

Sarah saw that several of the tavern's patron's looked over at her friend, but they turned back with disappointment when Nadia didn't do any more of a dance to the fiddle, instead making a beeline for the door.

Sarah and Ellie hurried to join their friend, and then Nadia led them across the street and into the hatmaker's shop.

Sarah beamed. "'Tis a good notion ye hae. Everyone here wears fancy hats. Did ye notice?"

"Aye," said Ellie, absentmindedly wrapping one of her red curls around her finger while she looked at all the hats on the counters, and all the strange tools and bits of felt and leather on the shelves.

"Ah, first time in the city?" asked the elderly male hatmaker with a greedy gleam in his eye.

With a sinking feeling, Sarah approached him. "Aye, and we dinna hae much money. We wish tae bide in toon a bit and enjoy the sights, and we dinna hae time tae hae dresses made for us. Dae ye think we can afford used clothes that make us fit in here better with ye toon folk, some aught a connected person such as yourself might gather from his acquaintances? It need na be special, just more citified than oor farm attire." She opened her hand to reveal a silver coin.

The hatter put a spectacle in and looked at the

coin intently before answering her. "Where did three Highland lasses come intae such a fortune?"

Wait, one silver coin was a fortune?

Tall slender Nadia paused in her graceful sashay around the shop to raise her eyebrows at Sarah in an 'I told you so' look.

Sarah closed her hand and stepped back from the hatter. "Never ye mind. We wull be spending it elsewhere. Nadia, Ellie, we're leaving. We dinna need tae abide rudeness."

But the hatmaker held up his hands in supplication. "I pray ye forgive me, lass. I didna mean any disrespect. I greatly admire a Highland lass who comes intae a fortune, and o' course I would be verra pleased if ye would share it with me in exchange for using my connections tae acquire ready tae wear clothing suitable for the city."

Trying not to gloat, Sarah looked at her friends as if to consult with them on whether or not they should accept the man's apology.

Fully understanding what she was doing because she often held pretenses such as this in order to get them favors, they humored her and drew this out as long as possible, so that the shopkeeper could sweat a few moments. After about half a minute, they all nodded at each other.

Sarah turned back to the shopkeeper. "How long will it take ye, tae gather what is needed tae outfit all three o' us as befits lasses o' Inverness?"

Smiling to himself, the man took out a tape and went about measuring them from a distance, a process the three of them found very amusing. He wrote down the measurements on a chalkboard that sat on the counter with the tools and materials of his hat-making trade. "I wull close the shop and go about toon in the next hour. Should only take me that long tae gather everything. Please tell me that is satis-factory."

"'Tis," Sarah told him, moving toward the door and nodding her head for Nadia and Ellie to follow. "But we dinna wish tae sit here that long. As I said, we wish tae see the toon. We will return here afore we retire for the night."

The hatter reached out his hand toward Sarah's fist, where she held the silver coin.

But she made a tighter fist. "Nay. Ye shall na hae yer payment till we hae oor new toon clothing and hae satisfied ourselves it fits and is appropriate." She looked at the greedy gleam in his eye. "And ye shall give me change o' half a silver coin."

The gleam in his eye only reduced a small amount.

Darn, she should have asked for more change. Oh well. She had quite a bit of money in her bag, if this was any indication. Had Kelsey known?

They walked down the street, looking through the un-shuttered windows at the contents of all the shops. It was difficult not to exclaim about everything they saw —all handmade out of natural materials.

Nadia whispered to the two of them, "We should buy some o' this stuff, bring it home, and sell it. We could make a fortune."

"Ooh!" Ellie exclaimed in what was dangerously close to no longer being a whisper.

Sarah elbowed Ellie in the side but kept them walking and looking in the windows, whispering, "A good idea it may be, but look about at how the people here behave. Ye canna get sae excited, na about that nor anything. And I dinna think we should deal in antiques till we get a feel for the place. Dinna look now, but a man has been following us ever syne we left the inn."

Annoyingly, both of her friends looked around very obviously.

Fuming, Sarah grabbed their hands and dragged them into the nearest shop, which turned out to belong to a printer. It smelled like turpentine.

The printer smiled at them in greeting. "What can I help ye lasses with this day?"

Sarah lowered her voice so as not to be heard from outside. "There's a man following us. We just ducked in here for refuge."

The shopkeeper's lips formed a line on his face, and his eyes grew resolved. "Ye can leave oot the back door. I wull detain him."

"That's verra kind o' ye. We wull."

They rushed out the back door, down the alley, and into the shop across the street.

"What wondrous clothing ye make!" Sarah told the female shopkeeper as she gazed all around at the dresses in various stages of completion. "If I were tae get fitted right now, how long would it take for ye tae make me a dress?"

The shopkeeper made her way over to Sarah and started taking measurements. "If ye be truly rushit, I can hae some aught ready for ye by the end o' business tomorrow. But it will cost, ye ken."

Sarah beamed and showed the shopkeeper the silver coin, looking at all the bolts of fabric on the walls and letting her imagination run wild. "'Tis a deal ye hae. I simply love yer work."

"Which fabric dae ye like?"

"I love that gray there."

The shopkeeper got it down and draped it over Sarah in various ways, pinning as she did so. After a long while, she indicated a raised area in the middle of the room. "Step up here."

Sarah did.

The dressmaker reviled them with talk as she pinned Sarah's hem. "'Tis glad I am, tae hae yer custom. Business has been sae bad syne the English passed their Alien Act. I dinna ken if ye heard about it out in the land, but here in toon 'tis all the talk. Those who own land in England are afraid their heirs will na inherit, and not a one wants tae go tae England tae try and sell their land. Put us in a bad way, it has..."

Nadia cleared her throat and used her fingers to comb her long brown hair back to reveal the need in her gray eyes. "'Tis sorry I am tae raise a delicate subject, but we had quite a bit o' ale with supper. Where is the nearest place that I might, ye ken, relieve myself?"

Ellie jumped up from the stool she was seated on, making her red curls bounce. "I will go with ye."

"Just oot my back door there," said the shop-keeper around the pins she had in her mouth.

"Wait till I can go as wull," Sarah practically yelled.

"Come on, Sarah," said Ellie. "I aim tae be as ladylike as I can, but ye canna expect me tae hold it for another half hour while ye get fitted for a dress ye dinna need. We will be just ootside there," she turned to the shopkeeper, "aye?"

The woman nodded impatiently, grabbing onto Sarah's waist to steady her. "Stand still, or I canna guarantee the dress will fit."

Sarah's friends went out the back door.

She tried to relax and enjoy having a dress custom made, but she worried too much. "I'm anxious for my friends," she told the shopkeeper as she stripped off the fabric, cursing every few seconds when a pin stuck her. "They're younger than I, ye ken, and they hae never been tae the city afore. They dinna ken about all the dangers. Besides, a man was following us. That's why we rushed in here. I hae tae go check on them."

After grabbing her leather backpack and putting it on one shoulder, Sarah jumped down and ran to the back door, pushing it open with her rump when it stubbornly stuck to the frame. The sun had set, and she had to squint to see in the moonlight after being under the bright lamps inside.

At first she didn't notice the privy in the alley-way, it looked so much like a storage crate. But her anxiety grew even upon seeing it. Surely both her friends couldn't fit in there?

A distant scream cut through the air but a moment before it was stifled.

Sarah whipped her head to the left to look down the alley — where her friends were both gagged and in the arms of that man who had been following them.

Sarah ran through the shop and out the front door, ignoring the shopkeeper's cry of "Dae ye still want the dress?"

She ran all the way back to the inn, up the stairs, and into the room Meehall had rented, out of breath and scrambling in her backpack for the bracer to put on her arm and then finally sighing in relief when the world started whirling and she made her way back to Celtic University in modern times.

4

Helping out with the sword-fighting class had been a good idea. Some of the students were even a challenge, and Meehall encouraged them to give him a strong workout. His current sparring partner was especially tough, having 50 pounds more muscle than him. Meehall's technique was better, honed by years of actual battle experience, but the man's strength was nothing to be dismissed. One solid hit would have Meehall on the floor. Dancing away from the hits allowed him to work out his anger in a productive manner.

Meehall's youngest brother, John (*Eoin* \OAÑ\ in Gaelic), had shown up in 1704 two years ago, saying things hadn't worked out back in the time of

Hadrian's Wall. They hadn't seen each other for awhile, so it was good to catch up on all the happenings. There were ways he could call on his brother for help getting back to 1706, so Meehall wasn't entirely out of luck.

But the idea of being rescued by a younger brother grated. No, Meehall wasn't that desperate yet. He would give Sarah a day to come back before he lowered himself to asking his younger brother for help.

The giant slammed down a particularly hard attack, forcing Meehall to run.

Watching the sword rather than where he was going, he backed right into someone. "Sorry," he said, eyes still on the sword.

"Are you okay?" Sarah asked, doubtlessly dazzled by the giant's size.

Good, she was back already. And she had his bracer.

Meehall gave his opponent the signal that their bout was over and waited, eyes never leaving that sword.

The burly man acknowledged the signal, sheathed his sword, and wiped his forehead with a towel. "Good bout, mate."

Meehall shook hands with the man, then turned

to Sarah, reluctant to let her know how relieved he was to see her. "Sarah! How about we show these students how it's done?" He grabbed a quarterstaff for her from the rack as he searched around for a likely pair of opponents.

But she stayed his hand when he started to beckon. "I'm way out of practice—"

Good. That'll teach her a lesson about running off with my bracer, even if Kelsey and Stanley are really to blame. "Let's remedy that right away." He tossed her the staff.

She caught it but then put it away. "I don't have time to practice—"

Really? That was her excuse? "I'm so glad you came back from your trip early. I really need to go on a trip of my own, and with us sharing a ...vehicle—"

Sarah's eyes said she didn't want to hear it. Too bad.

Needing to get her alone so he could speak freely, he put a hand on her lower back without a second thought and escorted her out of the gymnasium into the cool night air, where he wiped the sweat off his face with one of his billowing Highlander sleeves.

She went with him eagerly. Weird.

Might as well make the best of it. "Thank you for

coming back early, Sarah. I really appreciate it." His hand on her back began to feel forward, and he lowered it, but not before their eyes met and a familiar hunger arose in him. That wasn't meant to be, so he fought it down.

But Sarah didn't turn away. "I'm going with you. My friends Nadia and Ellie went with me, and they have been kidnapped back in 1706." She ran toward Stanley's office.

He caught up and ran alongside her. "Give back my bracer."

"I will, once we're back in 1706."

"Okay," he sighed in annoyance.

5

"How thin are the walls here?" Sarah asked as soon as they were in Meehall's room at the inn. She had his full attention now, and it was unnerving. Feeling his hand on the small of her back at the sword practice and again in Stanley's office had been bad enough, but his eyes boring into hers? She wanted to look away. Wanted to with all of her reason. But she needed him.

"They wull dae," he told her thoughtfully. But he switched on the TV and turned the news announcer up a little. "Explain tae me what happened, sae I wull hae a better idea where tae look for the lasses."

It was too close, being with him in a bedroom. Far too tempting to do things she knew she'd regret. He wasn't dependable, best she remember that. She headed for the door. "I wull just show ye. 'Twill be quicker and more accurate. Besides, ye might see something that gives ye a clue."

"Sarah." He grabbed her hand before she could reach the doorknob.

This was too much. She gave him her icy stare. "What?"

"My bracer."

His proximity clouded her brain. "Oh, aye. Canna wander aboot with this on. Who kens when I might disappear back tae Celtic?" She tried a light-hearted laugh, but it sounded shrill.

Heart aflutter, it was all she could do to open her pack on the bed, gingerly take off the bronze bracer, and put it inside. All she wanted to do was pull him down on top of her and...

"Nay, ye promised tae ..."

She couldn't look at him as she closed up her pack and put it back on. "What?"

"Never ye mind. Times are different, as ye ken, sae if the two o' us come oot o' this room together, we had best tell people ye are my wife."

"Fine. I dinna hae a mind tae speak with anyone anyhow."

"Even still."

She stared at his hand holding hers.

"I wull let go," he said, "when ye agree tae act like we are marrit —in front o' others."

She huffed to cover her blush and the trembling of her hand. "Verra wull. Now unhand me."

He did, and then he opened the door and gestured for her to precede him out.

She had to hand it to him, he'd always been a gentleman. At least in his mannerisms, if not in keeping his word. The more important part.

Fortunately, no one spoke to them on their way out into the dark street, lit only by the light coming out through the curtained windows. The hatmaker's shop was closed, they walked to the next street, then crossed to the other side and entered the dressmaker's shop.

"I was beginning tae think ye would na return. Tell me, dae ye want the dress, or nay?"

Unsure what to say, Sarah looked to Meehall for help.

He put his hand on the small of her back. "'Tis sorry we are for any trouble tae ye, howsoever, my wife's friends were kidnapped this day. Can ye show me where they went when they were separated from her?"

Anger flared in the shopkeeper's face, and Sarah

was relieved. She'd expected a scene, but now it appeared they were going to get help.

"I sent them oot my back door tae the privy." She put down her sewing and got up to lead the way. "Just oot here."

Meehall kept his hand on Sarah's back the whole time he escorted her out into the alley. "I thank ye," he said to the shopkeeper with a sincere dip of his chin. "Please, gae back tae business. We wullna keep ye any longer."

Sarah felt guilty. "Finish the dress," she told her with what she hoped was a placating smile, holding out the silver coin. "I took far tae much o' yer time not tae give ye my custom."

The shopkeeper took it, giving them both a graceful smile. "Grateful I am, that ye could think o' me in a time o' such distress. Here's hoping ye find the lasses."

"Did ye see the man who was following us when we first entered yer shop?"

"Aye, that I did. 'Twas Coll Cameron."

Meehall's hand on her back tensed. "We canna waste any time. We must get Smoke and ride for the Cameron camp."

The shopkeeper led them back through her shop, moving things out of their way. "Godspeed."

Meehall took off running. "There is na time tae waste. The lasses will be forced tae wed Camerons. I hae tae rescue them straight away. I wull ride tae their camp, sneak in and grab them, and ride out."

Sarah ran to keep up with him as they approached the inn. "I'm going with ye, or how wull ye ken 'tis my friends?"

As they ran, he lowered his face at her as if to say 'Really? How stupid do you think I am? Two modern women will stand out among the people of this time.' But out loud he only said, "I feared ye would says sae."

They had arrived at the inn's stable door.

He opened it and gestured for her to precede him into the darkness.

She went in and quickly moved aside to make room for him.

A yawning stable boy brought Smoke out.

Meehall's horse was a large gray who danced in place, he was so impatient to get on the road.

Sarah went digging in her bag for the money purse, saying to the stable hand, "I wish tae hire a horse for myself, a gentle mare."

But Meehall stayed her hand. "My wife will ride with me." He held her wrist with one hand while helping the boy tack up the horse with the other.

Sarah tried to jerk free of his hold, but it was firm. Their struggle made her bag tilt to the side. This revealed a glimpse of the bracer, which caught the lamplight and shined for a moment, glinting there. She jerked the bag to make the lid come down and then put it firmly on her shoulder.

But Meehall had seen. He glanced significantly down at the force he was using to hold onto her wrist, up at her bag, and then into her eyes.

His resolute stare infuriated her mind, but it was making her body react in ways she would rather it didn't.

He lowered his head to her ear and breathed for only her to hear, "Out of respect for you, I won't just take it, but there's a limit." He drew away and then said for the stable boy's ears as well, "This is na a pleasure ride, Sarah. We wull get there faster if I dinna hae tae guide ye."

"But..." Sarah couldn't say what she was thinking in front of the stable boy. He was young, and only his parents should tell him about such things. But she met Meehall's eyes and let him see the reluctance in her face.

He shrugged dramatically. "That's one of the things you should consider before you insist upon coming along." He gave her that resolute stare again, the one that had made her resist riding horseback with him in the first place. "'Twould be best if ye bided here at the inn."

"I am na gaun'ae dae that."

"Then ye are gaun'ae ride with me."

He and the stable hand were done saddling the horse, and Meehall climbed up, eyes now resentfully on her pack that contained the bracer, letting her know in no uncertain terms that her possession of it was the only reason he didn't just charge off without her.

She reached for him to help her up. "I canna bide here with my friends oot wondering why I dragged them intae this."

He pointed at her backpack. "Close that bag properly, and put it firmly on ye. Tie the straps."

She did as he said, looking down to hide the flush that rose in her cheeks. How could she have been so careless with the bracer?

He reached down and helped her up, seating her behind him and putting her arms firmly around his waist while speaking to the stableboy. "Tell Master Neil we wull return on the morrow, and tae please hold a room for us." He held out a copper coin.

The stable boy took the coin and bowed his head, then ran off through the door to the inn.

Being this close to Meehall was just as torturous as Sarah had feared it would be. He felt so good. He always had. As if she belonged next to him. And she couldn't shrink away from his touch, because the horse felt lively under her, like a motorcycle that would take off at full speed any second.

They rode in silence through the dark streets of Inverness, still bustling with people. There were several taverns here on the main road and the people walked to and fro from one to another.

But once they had ridden through the city gate onto the highway, the night was deserted. Not even the stars could be seen under Scotland's cloudy sky.

It was chilly, and Sarah found herself clinging to Meehall for warmth as well.

Every few steps, the horse would try and take off running, perhaps sensing their need for urgency.

But Meehall reined him in.

Sarah couldn't take it anymore. "Why dae ye na let him run?"

"'Tis a long way, and even a horse grows weary. Nay, we wull arrive sooner if he walks."

"How long will it take?"

"We wull be there afore morning."

"Dae ye think they'll be marrit off in the night?"

"Nay."

For awhile, the only sound was the clopping of the horse's hooves.

"Listen," Meehall said to the night in front of him, "I would never have left you under ordinary circumstances, Sarah. But it was for your own good—"

"Kelsey told me already."

Was she imagining it, or had his breathing sped up? More importantly, why did she care? She needed to think about something else.

But the only other thing on her mind was fear for her friends. What must they be going through? Imagining their tear-streaked faces brought tears to her own eyes —and sobs to her chest. This was her fault. Her selfishness had caused her friends misery. Why had she insisted on time traveling and bringing them with her?

Meehall's voice was less haughty and more compassionate. "When we get there, you stay on Smoke. He'll protect you if ... need be. You hear?"

Too racked with sobs now to speak, Sarah nodded her head against his back, using the movement to wipe some of her tears away.

"Good. I'm thriving here in this time. I like it far better than modern life, but—"

"Shut up, Michael. Just shut up."

❧ 6 ❧

In the black of night, Meehall stopped Smoke on top of the ridge over Cameron camp, gave his horse the pat that said 'hold still until told otherwise,' and climbed down, leaving Sarah in the saddle alone. "If the Camerons find ye, ride away tae safety. Dinna stop till ye are back inside the gates o' Inverness."

She started to object. He could see it in the way her eyes sparkled, the way she cocked her head to the side, the sharp breath she took.

He grabbed hold of her knee and shook it, stroking Smoke's neck to keep the horse still. "Heed me, Sarah. There are na police in this time. If the Camerons find ye, ye must needs go back tae the inn and use the bracer tae return home. Tell Kelsey what happened. She wull ken what tae dae. Give me yer word ye wull heed this."

She swallowed, and tears fell from her eyes as she winced down at him from Smoke's calm and steady back. "This is all getting tae much for my heart tae take, Meehall. Would that we had called upon Kelsey tae begin with."

"Aboot that," he said frankly, now gripping her knee in earnest while he rested a calming hand on Smoke's nose. "I was na comfortable with Kelsey at oor private lunch yesterday. She looked at me the way the druids dae, ye ken? As if she could see my whole life playing oot before her. She has taken on their airs as wull. I am telling ye, oor friend bides inside her head somewhere, but she has become one o' them. I dinna trust her."

Sarah's tears flowed freely now, dripping off her cheeks and falling down onto her dark woolen skirts.

She wiped her nose with the back of her hand. "I dae ken. Hoping, I was, that it was just my own notion. But now I ken ye hae the right o' it." She hastily took off her backpack, no small feat on horseback and holding the reins. "Here, I can offer ye a wee bit o' help. This fancy bag o' modern wonders is from the place where Lauren worked, back in oor time. Kelsey gave it to me just last week, sae she isna all gone, I dinna think. Take this. 'Tis one o' those emergency signal lights backpackers take intae the wild. 'Tis a verra bright light, and nay one here wull be expecting that." She handed him what looked like a thick pen.

"My thanks. It just may come in handy." He played with it for a moment, turning the strobe off and on, and when he was confident he could work it, put it in his sporran. He then trailed his hand along Smoke's side while he walked back to the saddlebags. "Caress his neck, Sarah. 'Twill keep him calm."

She did as he asked, surprising him by keening to Smoke as she did. Pretty effectively, too, even if it did sound like she was petting a dog. "There's a good boy. Yeah. Yer staying still, are ye na?"

He got his sword belt down and strapped it on over his kilt. "We wull be in a grand hurry when I return, sae let us now work oot who wull walk and who wull ride, and where. Yer friends are na fat, are they?"

Sarah laughed, and because she was still crying, her eyes sparkled like diamonds in the faint moonlight that managed to sneak down through the thick Scottish clouds. "Nay, neither o' them weighs much more than 100 pounds. The four o' us on Smoke will weigh nay more than two large men."

His hand moved to pat her knee in sympathy, but he resisted the urge to touch her again. "Wull enough. Here I go. Be ready. Put yer pack on the front o' ye." He waited while she did it. "Aye. I wull hand them up tae sit behind ye. I wull run."

She was trembling, but her tears had slowed.

Good. He needed her to have her head about her.

"Godspeed, Michael."

"I wull see ye afore long," he said as he turned around and headed for the steep trail he had made.

Aye, he had crept in among the Camerons before, to spy on them. They weren't nearly as careful as they should be with the side of their camp that was up against the mountain. Climbing down from above it was difficult, to be sure —he hoped the lasses would be able to manage, come to think of it— but it was doable. Eminently doable. Even in the dark, like now.

There weren't any fires in the camp. All were abed then, all who would be.

He was tempted to use the signal light to help him see. It was such a fun gadget, and he hadn't had much chance to play with gadgets these past eight years.

But he might as well put a big floating arrow over

his head, saying 'Here I am! Come get me, ye Camerons!' So he painstakingly climbed down in the dark until he got to the edge of the camp and heard people snoring inside their tents.

Wait. Now that he was down here and no longer exerting himself to climb, he heard people talking. Who would be the only ones up this late? The guards. The ones who were guarding the lasses.

He crept through the camp toward the voices.

Lest anyone come out in need of relieving themselves, he always kept in mind where he would run and hide if that should happen. There was nothing specific about his apparel that would give him away, but the clan was small enough that they would recognize him as a stranger right off, even in the dark.

At long last, he came upon the lasses. Foolish Camerons. They had placed their captive brides near the base of the mountain, on the opposite end of the camp from where he'd come down. There was another way up not far from here.

Now, all he had to do was sneak up behind the guards and knock them out, untie the lasses from each other's backs, and help them climb up to Sarah and Smoke.

He snuck around some bushes and readied the end of his sword to strike both men in the head.

He paused. The guards were ten feet away. Before he got to them, the lasses would surely notice him.

He put his finger over his lips and, praying the lasses would keep quiet and not give his presence away, he crept out from behind the bushes.

The one lass with the red hair and freckles saw him first. Good lass. She fell over on her side away from him, taking the other lass with her.

The other lass groaned at thudding upon the ground, drawing the attention of their guards.

Both men quit talking and looked down at the lasses.

Meehall made his move. After getting close enough to knock the one guard out, he raised his sword to strike the other.

But the Cameron who remained standing opened his mouth to yell.

Meehall covered the man's mouth with his hand, but in order to do this, he had to drop his sword.

The Cameron got in a good blow to Meehall's head.

Meehall wrestled him to the ground and subdued him, but he heard the camp rousing. He only had a few seconds before people would be here. He grabbed his sword, ran to the lasses, and used it to cut their bonds, whispering as he did, "We hae tae climb the cliff. Sarah is up there with the horse. We dinna hae any time tae lose, sae stay with me, ye ken?"

They both nodded fiercely, the one helping ungag the other.

He moved briskly toward the other trail, the more difficult one.

The lasses hurried after him.

They had gone thirty feet up when an arrow whizzed past his head.

"Go on, keep climbing," he told the lasses as he took out the strobe light and set it to not blink. He turned it on and aimed it where the arrow had come from, moving it around so that the impossibly bright light shone everywhere, hopefully making his enemies night blind.

Cameron cries of alarm pleased him immensely.

This part of the trail at the beginning was the hardest part though, and the lasses were having a lot of trouble finding hand and footholds in the dark.

"Would it be easier on ye if I went ahead tae show the way?"

"Aye," said the redhead. Ellie, from Sarah's description.

He made his way up past them. "The right hand

goes here, and then the right foot here, ye see?" He turned his head to check for understanding.

And then two Cameron men who obviously had not gotten the light in their faces popped up right behind the lasses, grabbed them, and carried them toward the camp down the steep trail.

The lasses kicked and fought, but they screamed too, no doubt waking the entire camp.

Why had he not seen that coming? Of course he hadn't night blinded all the Camerons.

Meehall cursed, and then he yelled down to the lasses, "We wull return for ye. On my word."

There were fires in the camp now, so he could see the lasses being tied up once more. He could also see that more men were on their way up the hill after him.

Meehall cursed all the way up to the top of the mountain.

"Sarah! Sarah, over here!"

There were hoofbeats, but they sounded too far away. He ran in their direction, and just when he thought she was going to be too late and the Camerons were going to catch up behind him, she appeared.

She looked horrified.

He held up his hands to soothe her. "I had yer

friends, Sarah. I had them freed, and they are wull." He climbed up on Smoke behind her, in the spot meant for her friends. "Not injured in the least. But then I lost them again. I'm sae sorry, Sarah."

Being surprisingly gentle to him who had disappointed her so, she pulled his arms tightly around her.

"What are ye on aboot?"

"'Tis naught," she said, but he could tell she was lying.

"I will na play this game with ye, Sarah. I ken ye wull tell me eventually."

This side of the mountain sloped much more gradually, and she coaxed Smoke into a canter, sensibly putting more distance between them and the Camerons.

He made his voice as contrite as he could, under the circumstances. "Ye must hae taken riding lessons since the last time we spoke. Ye are handling Smoke wull."

"Thanks," she breathed out between hoofbeats. "He's a great horse. I only hae tae nudge, and he does what I want."

They had come enough distance now that no one would catch them on foot.

He took the reins in front of her hands and

slowed Smoke to a walk. "Most o' the horses in this time are like this. They dinna stand aboot all the live-long day like horses in oor time."

"Are Ellie and Nadia well? They didna... The men didna hurt them, did they?"

"Nay, nay they're wull."

Something was dripping down his face. Annoyed, he shrugged up his arm to wipe it. And saw blood on his sleeve.

At the same time, what Sarah had asked him to try and do became difficult.

Sleep was taking him.

"Come tae think on it, I wull take a wee nap," he said, nodding off against Sarah's back. "We need tae go tae Murray camp and get more people. Head through that pass." He guided her sight along his arm and pointed. "Ciaran and Baltair will help us."

She groaned.

Vaguely aware of her reining Smoke in, he roused a bit. "Ye canna stop. Ye must keep on, or they wull catch us."

She turned in the saddle and started unbuckling his belt, her face intent on the task.

"Aw, 'tis na the time, Sarah."

Rolling her eyes, she fastened his belt to the

saddle. "Ye canna hold on if ye are sleeping, now can ye?"

"I suppose not."

She tore a strip from her arisade and tied it round and round his head, then pulled his arms tightly around her again, but this time she tied them together at the wrists with a soft cord from inside her pack.

And just in time, because darkness took him as he collapsed against her back.

7

Through the rest of the night, Sarah clung to Meehall's arm with her left hand while she held the reins with her right. She was guiding Smoke toward the path whenever he wandered too far, but letting the horse have his head most of the time. He was far more experienced at trudging through the Highlands that she was.

The sun came up, and that was a relief. Although she had led her friends on an adventure only to have it turned into a nightmare for them, at least she wasn't going to fall off a horse that tripped over something in the dark.

She got hungry and munched an energy bar from her fancy backpack, worried about Meehall. Did he have a concussion?

This was stupid. She should just use the bracer and take him back to the 21st Century.

But as soon as she stopped Smoke, Meehall roused. "Canna trust Kelsey. Keep going through the pass. Need tae go see Eoin." He slumped back against her back, snoring.

Well, if he was coherent enough to talk, then she supposed he didn't have a concussion. That was good. Hopefully he would just sleep it off and be good as new.

Doubt gripped her again when she got to a roaring river. How on earth did you cross one of these things without a bridge? She stopped Smoke again and looked to the left and the right. She didn't see any sign that the river got shallower.

Once again, Meehall roused enough to speak. His groggy voice came close behind her ear. "Fill this with water."

She followed his gaze back to a bladder skin peeking out of the saddlebags, grabbed it, and handed him an energy bar as she got down to fill it.

He rasped in her ear again after they had both drunk their fill and she was once more mounted in front of him. "The crossing is doon river. About a mile. After ye cross, gae doon another half-mile and ye wull find the pass." He slumped against her back and re-commenced snoring.

Near the top of the pass, Sarah heard voices. And smelled cows. She stopped Smoke so she could listen.

And again Meehall roused. How he could sleep with the horse moving but was woken up by its stillness baffled her.

Nonetheless, his voice once again came to her ear. "'Tis the Gordons ye hear. Friends, na foes. Gae on."

When she rounded the next bend in the canyon, she saw a sizable camp. There was even a building up here, at the cross of the Ridge Road and the Canyon Road.

"Aye," said Meehall, "head for the inn."

An inn sounded wonderful. At this point she'd been awake 32 hours.

Two huge kilted men came out of the building and ran over.

"Meehall Murray, what has befallen ye?"

"Step doon, lass, and let us give ye aid."

More than willing to let them handle the horse

and get Meehall into a room inside the one building, she slid down —and almost fell, she was so saddle sore. Meehall wasn't walking too well, either. She was glad a beefy Highlander was helping him climb the stairs and then lowering him onto a bed in one of the two inn rooms upstairs.

The Gordans were probably wondering who she was, and she didn't want to damage his reputation. "We were marrit yesterday—"

From where he lay on the bed, Meehall cut her off with surprising quickness and lucidity. "Aye, and we wish tae be left alone. I thank ye, Gordon lads."

The 200-pound 'lads' laughed heartily at this and excused themselves, closing the door behind them.

Meehall groaned. "We stopped here for rest, Sarah, na tae tell the Gordons oor business." He closed his eyes and was almost immediately snoring again.

Sarah got a good look at him then, and gasped. Why was she thinking of arguing when his head bandage was crusted with blood?

She washed his wound with the soap and water in a bowl and pitcher on top of the dresser, dried it with the clean part of her leine on the inside of her skirts, and then dressed it with antibiotic salve from the first-aid kit in her backpack. His wound could use stitches, but she didn't dare try that. It was better off left to heal on its own, even even if it did leave a scar.

Anyway, guys liked having scars. She fondly remembered Meehall showing off the scar under his chin the first day she met him.

"I got this from a swordfight," he'd said, proudly puffing out his 13-year-old chest. He'd been an adorable 13-year-old, athletic and smiling.

Gazing over his form, she realized he was a gorgeous 25-year-old now, athletic and... fast asleep. Laugh lines were starting to form at the sides of his mouth and in the corners of his eyes. The sun had bronzed his skin so that his blue eyes, when open, seemed especially merry.

And she could tell he was sorry for leaving her by the way those blue eyes pleaded with her. It was a relief not to have to look into them now.

Right. And she shouldn't be so close to him. It would give their bodies the wrong idea, and a few desperate lonely experiences had taught her it wasn't worth it, getting close to someone you didn't plan on spending the rest of your life with.

No, that armchair over there was where she should sleep.

There was a knock at the door, and she got up, cracked it open, and peeked out.

A girl no more than 13 years old gave her a brief curtsy, making her long woolen skirts crumple on the polished wooden floor. "I brought up some food, for ye and yer husband." Handing over a cloth-wrapped bundle, she dipped again and then went back downstairs.

Curious, Sarah opened the bundle. Inside, she found bread, meat, and cheese. All the makings for sandwiches, but nothing to cut them with.

Meehall's voice drifted up from the bed before she was able to say anything. "My knife is sheathed in my right boot. And dinna ye crack any jokes aboot cutting the cheese. My head ails me already, and I can only assume laughter would make it worse."

She found the knife, prepared the food, and gave him some. They ate in silence. There was a skin of weak wine in the bundle as well, and they both drank their fill.

Sarah had just squirted the last of this into her mouth when it occurred to her. "They dinna hae Porta Potties here like at the faire."

Meehall barked one note of a laugh before groaning. "I telt ye nay tae make me laugh. Use that pot in the corner. Let me hae another little nap, and then we wull gae home tae my clan and get help."

"Sounds good," she told him.

He patted the bed next to him.

But she once again chose the armchair.

❧

WHEN SHE AWOKE NEEDING THE POT, IT WAS dark again. She groaned. "I dinna want tae stumble aroond oot there again."

"I agree," said Meehall in a voice that was awake enough to be relieving. "We wull hae tae stay the night. I smell supper downstairs. Are ye hungry?"

"Aye."

The tavern downstairs was full of Gordons, but Sarah and Meehall found seats at the end of the bench nearest the kitchen. The first few minutes, all she did was eat and listen. The beef stew was good, and the talk among the Gordons was interesting, similar to what she'd heard in Inverness.

"We canna allow oorselves tae be bound tae the English. We must needs bide on oor own."

"We thought there was a way. Scotland sent all oor money off tae Caledonia. We squandered it."

"We did na. The filthy rich did."

Sarah thought they could use a change of subject, to a common cause. She gestured to Meehall's now scabbed head wound. "The Camerons did this tae him. We—"

Before she knew what was happening, Meehall had his hand over her mouth and his other arm around her, lifting her up over the bench. "My wife does na ken when tae keep silent. We wull take the rest o' oor supper up in oor room. Please tell the serving lass, wull ye?"

One of the two huge Highlanders who had heard about their desire to be alone nodded yes with far too much amusement in his eyes. "Ye wull teach her who is the man, I reckon."

"Aye," said Meehall as he hauled her up the stairs, "that I wull."

As soon as they were in their room and the door was closed, Sarah seethed at him. "Certies if we tell the Gordons oor friends were kidnapped, they wull help. Why did ye hae tae embarrass me?"

Meehall's face was inches from her own. His blue eyes were flashing with anger. He seethed back at her. "'Tis tae dangerous, Sarah. Nadia and Ellie are modern lasses. The Gordons would wonder at them, especially if they were the center o' attention after being the subject o' such a large undertaking.

We canna risk it. I only trust my own clan with such a matter."

How dense could he be?

"Tae dangerous tae go rescue them? 'Tis tae dangerous not tae! My friends are in captivity, and 'tis my fault! We hae tae get them oot o' there."

"Aye, 'tis yer fault. But 'tis na my fault. I'm gang doon tae hae the rest o' my supper. Ye hae my bracer. Ye should use it. Gae haime. Let my clan handle the rescue."

"Gang tae yer clan wull only cause more delay. I wull gae get Kelsey. She wull ken what tae dae, and she can bring—"

He again put a hand over her mouth. "Nay, I telt ye, we canna trust Kelsey. Eoin has this time travel ring. I wull gae tae him. He and the clan wull help me rescue the lasses, and then he can return them tae their time. Ye dinna need tae be along," He had turned away from her and was already through the door and closing it. What she hadn't expected was to hear a bar come down over the outside of the door. She was locked in the room.

"Ye should na be drinking!" she yelled after him. "Dinna forget yer head injury,"

"Quiet, Sarah!" was all he said before laughter came up from the tavern.

She was seeing red. What was she supposed to do in here all by herself? There was no way she could sleep, she was so angry. If she took off these skirts, she could do some jumping jacks. That might help.

She had the overskirt halfway off when there was a knock at the door.

Which meant the door was unbarred.

She could go down there and invite the Gordons to come help them rescue Nadia and Ellie from the Camerons after all! She hurriedly put her skirt and backpack back on, threw open the door, and—

But the serving girl had the two big beefy Highlanders with her.

Sarah took her bowl of stew and closed the door as graciously as she could. She wasn't going anywhere. All she could do was hope she could get Meehall to rescue her friends soon, so she wouldn't have to deal with him anymore.

8

Meehall held his tankard out for the serving lass to refill with ale.

Angus stopped his hand when he tried to pay. "Ye got the last two rounds. This one is mine."

Emil clinked tankards with his brother. "'Tis all the rounds we should be getting. He's having wife trouble."

They both laughed, but it wasn't unkind.

Emil sat back in his chair and studied Meehall over the rim of his tankard. "Besides, yer wife does hae the right o' it. Ye should help her get her clanswomen back as soon as ye are able."

Meehall threw his hand up. "Ye canna expect me tae go again alone."

Emil shook his head, making his long red hair sway about. "Nah, but we can expect ye tae take us in the place o' yer clan. Sae ye can leave for Cameron camp on the morrow."

Angus clinked his brothers tankard again. "Aye. Ye insult us with the idea that the Murrays fight any better than the Gordons."

Meehall gave them his best 'oh, come on' look.

But Emil and Angus were now drawing other Gordons in.

"'Tis two days' ride tae Murray camp, and two day back again, and that does na even count the time tae get from here tae Cameron camp. Six days 'twould be in all, when he has fine Gordon fighters here and now."

"And 'tis na like the Camerons wull go all oot tae keep two lasses. Once they see oor Gordon might, they wull give up the lasses withoot a fight, mind ye."

※

IN THE END, MEEHALL HAD TO GIVE IN AND agree to leave for Cameron camp with the Gordons in the morning. "Sarah wull be glad upon it. I wull gae tell her the news."

Angus clapped him on the back. "Yer night wull be much better for it as wull, eh?"

I wish. Wait, do I?

When had that happened? He took the stairs two at a time. He couldn't even wait until he was done unbarring the door to tell her. "Sarah, I changed my mind. The Gordons are gaun'ae help us rescue Nadia and Ellie—" Funny, he had taken the bar off the door, but it still wasn't opening. "Sarah?"

No answer.

Aw, that was good. She wasn't there. She had used the bracer as he had recommended. She would be safe.

He turned to yell down the staircase but then realized he couldn't tell anyone she had vanished. He would have to climb up into the bedroom from outside in the morning to retrieve the things he had left in the room.

He would just sleep on the floor in the dark end of the hallway and hope no one discovered him. He sure wished he at least had his cloak to pad the floor with.

This was better anyway. He wouldn't need to see her again until he was able to return her friends to the 21st Century, with Eoin's help.

Sarah was waiting for him when he rode back into Murray camp with the other warriors, exuberant at their victory. She and Malina embraced him and Eoin, and they all went to the feast together, happy faces lit up by the bonfire.

Sarah held his hand all the while, gently squeezing it whenever she found someone's jest particularly funny. He anticipated which jests those would be with great accuracy, he knew her so well.

Their two sons played nearby. Irv and Hamish were good lads, obedient to their clan and eager to help with the chores. Meehall was proud of them.

After the feasting was over, he took Sarah's hand, caressing as he did so, and helped her up, leading her out onto the moor under the starry sky. They walked arm in arm then, far enough away from everyone where it wasn't unseemly.

She gazed up at the sky in awe and wonder. "I never dreamed I would see sae many stars."

Something about her comment was odd, but he

couldn't dwell on that now. Not with the starlight reflecting in her eyes and the gentle breeze lilting her hair around her face just so. "Sarah."

She took her gaze down from the stars to look at him. It was plain she enjoyed what she saw. Her face relaxed into one of invitation.

He accepted, pulling her close and lifting her face by the chin with his fingertips, kissing her as softly as the wind caressed her hair.

She rested her head against his neck, put her arms around him, and caressed his back as if they hadn't been living this way every day for the past ten years. I love ye, Meehall."

He choked up. He didn't understand why, but there it was. "Och, Sarah. Ye hae tae ken I love ye. If I dinna tell ye every day, then 'tis a poor husband I am, indeed."

There were tears in her eyes, but she was smiling, keeping her arms around his neck and pulling back to look at him. "Ye are the best husband. I could na ask for better. Ye make me verra happy, Meehall."

He was choking up even more, and he clung to her, desperate to show her how much she had moved him. "And ye are the best wife ever. I could na be more happy."

They stood there gazing at the starry sky together for a few moments more, and then she shivered, He escorted her to their tent in the camp and pulled the door open for her to go in before him.

They were in bed together before he knew what happened.

&

It was barely light when he awoke. Needing to relieve himself, he leaned over to give Sarah a peck on the cheek —and saw a wooden floor and wall where he expected to see his and Sarah's tent in Murray camp.

What the?

And then it came to him. That had all been a dream. Sarah was back in the 21st Century. And he needed to rescue her friends. Good, no one had disturbed him, so no one had seen him sleeping out here in the hallway outside his room at Gordon inh. He wouldn't have to explain.

He crept to the end of the hallway and peeked down the stairs. Still dark down there. Not even the kitchen fires were burning.

The stairs creaked. This was stupid. A warrior shouldn't sneak.

So what if he was seen going outside? He would say he was checking on Smoke. Decision made, he held his head up high and marched down the stairs, and through the tavern to the front door —which was not barred from the inside, glory be.

The Gordon cattle stood motionless in the hills outside camp, and the slight moonlight that penetrated the clouds reflected off the white patches in their shaggy fur.

Smoke whinnied when Meehall entered the dark stable. For the first time ever, he was glad no stablehand ran out to greet him. Not bothering with the saddle, Meehall led his horse out around the back of the tavern and bade him stand against the wall so he could stand on his back and have something to lean on.

With a sigh of relief, he just barely was able to push open the shutters and crawl up into his room.

It was darker inside and took his eyes a few moments to adjust. When they did, he couldn't believe he saw Sarah lying there.

"Ye are quite resourceful," she said, smiling mischievously.

"And ye are some aught else again." He grabbed her wrist and brought her downstairs, out to Smoke, and with the horse into the stable. "I could hae fallen tae my death."

She crossed her arms and raised one eyebrow. "Aye? And what if the inn had caught fire? I could hae burned tae my death."

What was she talking about? "Ye fully ken I would na allow ye tae burn."

She turned her hand over the way a magician would when saying, 'Voila!' "And ye fully ken Smoke would na allow ye tae fall."

Rather than admit she had a point, he changed the subject. "I suppose ye heard then, aboot the Gordons gang with us tae rescue yer friends."

"Aye, and I also heard 'twas na yer idea."

He relaxed his grip on her wrist a little as he guided her back to the tavern door. "I could dae with a few hoors sleep in a bed instead o' on the floor." He gave her a look meant to shame her.

But she lowered her chin at him. "Ye had plenty o' sleep in a bed yesterday."

But it wasn't to be in any case. When they entered the tavern, the cooking fires were now lit, and several people were already drinking their morning ale — Angus and Emil among them.

Angus beckoned them over. "I see ye ken the

plan, Sarah. Dinna fash. We wull return yer clanswomen tae ye."

Emil scooted over and made room for them. "'Tis good tae see the two o' ye holding hands. We were a bit fashed ye would hae annulments after we saw ye sleeping in the hallway."

Everybody laughed. Including Sarah.

MEEHALL AND SMOKE HAD MADE THIS TRIP down to Cameron camp and back a few times, so there were no surprises for him along the way.

But every time he turned in the saddle to check on Sarah, he saw her smiling the slightest bit at the scenery. He'd long grown accustomed to the Highlands, and her delight at them despite her fear and guilt over her friends reminded him of one reason why he had settled here.

The Gordons had agreed they should approach Cameron camp from the other direction this time, the surprise of coming down from the mountain having been ruined. And so the path they took deviated a bit from the way they had come the night before. Instead of mostly mountains and one large river, this time they rode through forests and one large meadow.

When they were about an hour away from the Camerons, Meehall stopped Smoke and turned him to face the Gordons. "We wull be under watch soon."

Angus nodded his agreement, as did the other dozen Gordons who accompanied them.

Emil pulled his horse up next to Smoke. "We wull enter from the east, where 'tis mostly meadows and they canna get a good shot at us from the trees. If we all ride as a unit, we wull be more imposing than if we trickle in by ones and twos."

Meehall patted Emil's shoulder. "I thank ye for the solidarity. Such a show o' strength wull be enough for them tae release the lasses."

He felt Sarah squeezing him from behind and patted her on the thigh. "Truly, Sarah, two lasses are hardly worth spilling blood ower. Dinna fash."

He was fairly sure of what he said, but it was a tense ride through the meadow and up the slight hill before Cameron camp. He didn't see the watch, but he knew they were there. He refused to look this way and that. The Gordons were doing a great job at seeming resolute, unwavering, and he didn't want to put himself to shame in comparison.

They rode up over the hill as an imposing unit —

and found Cameron camp deserted. Not a tent could be seen, nor any people. Flat areas of grass assured him this was the place.

He rode around until he found the spot where the lasses had been tied together and where the three of them had gone up the cliff. This was the spot, but the Cameron clan had moved on.

Sarah was in tears. "Nadia! Ellie! Ye hae tae be here..."

Under the shade of a tree, he handed her down from Smoke's back and gave her the reins. "We wull find their tracks, Sarah. 'Tis na ower. Walk him aboot a bit, but ride away at the first sign o' any stranger."

Her eyes had been dead with despair, but when he said tracks, her face bloomed with hope. She clung to his hand.

He gave her hand a gentle squeeze before he went off to join the other Highlanders. She was counting on him. He couldn't let her down.

Meehall was decent at tracking, but Angus and Emil were better. He would've taken everyone directly south, as it was the easiest way to leave the cliffside, but Emil found the real trail. It went north, further up into the Highlands.

Sarah smiled tentatively at Meehall when he came back to get her. "Ye did find their trail. I can see it in yer face. Sorry I am tae hae doubted ye." She reached up.

He helped her mount behind him on Smoke, and they rode off with their new Gordon friends.

A hundred Camerons with as many horses and twice as many cattle left a heckuva trail, even though they had gone single file at first, in an attempt not to.

Angus took off ahead of them at a trot. "They are na long gone. We hae a chance o' catching up!"

They had trotted their horses almost as far as was prudent when they arrived in a large circle where the Camerons had all gathered around for rest.

Meehall checked along the perimeter for the footprints leading out, but couldn't find them. Telling himself to suck it up, He went to ask Emil which way.

But Angus and Emil and all the others were still going up and down the area, looking for even a single-file pathway out. They went over and over and over the area, breaking first for the noonday meal and then for supper. They spent hours looking for the way everyone had left here. But they found none. The Cameron clan had disappeared into thin air.

Sarah whispered in his ear, "How many Druids must they hae, tae travel with sae many people and horses and cattle? I did na ken there were sae many Druids in the waurld!"

"I dinna ken," he whispered back. "I hope Eoin wull ken how tae find them sae we dinna hae tae ask Kelsey."

From the way no one spoke of it, he knew the Gordons also suspected magic. But all they did was eventually grunt that it was time to go, they had been gone long enough from their own cattle and their own lasses.

The ride back to Gordon camp was less cheerful. There were no jokes, no laughter. Their camp that night didn't have any happy stories. They were all sad stories of loss and yearning.

Meehall shook forearms with Angus and Emil in front of the stable in Gordon camp the next day. "I thank ye for coming tae help us rescue my wife's clanswomen. The Gordons and the Murrays are on good terms, and I look forward tae the day we meet again."

Meehall jumped up on Smoke in front of Sarah, and off they went. The day's ride was full of practical conversation. How many provisions had she in her pack and he in his saddlebags. Whether she should ride in the front sometimes —which he allowed. How far they could ride before they had to walk

Smoke, and how far they needed to walk him before they could ride again. How many people were in Murray camp, the names of his sons and the prominent people she would meet in his clan.

But try as he might, Meehall couldn't get them to Murray camp in one day. The two of them had to make camp alone.

✿ 9 ✿

Sarah pulled a log up closer to Meehall's campfire and sat down, taking her backpack off so that she could rummage around inside. "I hae all the modern conveniences in this nifty pack Lauren's auld work gave Kelsey. All we need is boiling water." She filled the little one-cup teapot from the creek nearby and sat patiently waiting for the fire to burn down to coals.

"Oh?" He was trying not to sound excited, but he was.

She knew him. He normally was lithe and graceful, so the jerkiness of his motions as he added larger sticks to the fire gave him away.

"Aye," she said nonchalantly. It wouldn't do to let him see she enjoyed his delight in what she had brought. "I even hae fruit punch, if there's aught we can mix it in. I dinna think we should put sugar in the water skin." She rummaged around in her bag some more and came up with a collapsible plastic water bottle. "Perfect." She went and filled that in the stream as well, taking the opportunity to pet Smoke's neck as she passed him.

When she got back, Meehall had taken over her log.

"Hey, that's mine." She put her hands on her hips to make her indignation more convincing, when in reality she wanted nothing more right now than to go sit with him.

He scooted over absentmindedly while stirring the fire with a long stick. "Sae what are ye fixing for supper?" He was trying to be cheerful for her sake, she could tell, but his face was just as concerned about the disappearing Camerons as it had been earlier. Though now it was starting to glow handsomely from the fire in the dying sunlight.

"Well," she said, "Oor supper was gaun'ae be a surprise, but syne ye asked. We wull hae meat lovers' lasagna complete with dried garlic bread." She took out the individual serving packages and showed him the pictures.

He studied them. "PenUlt. That would be the outfit Lauren used tae work for?"

She tore her eyes away from his strong slender fingers to look where he was pointing. A logo. "Aye. I had na noticed."

He abruptly pulled away. "The coals are ready. Let us set that water tae boiling. I hae na tasted lasagna in quite a long time." He used the stick to make a relatively flat surface of the hottest coals.

She placed the small kettle on this surface. "Should na be long." The temptation to scoot over close to him was almost palpable, and she had to fight it every second, coming up with other places to put her hands besides near him, where he might take hold of them.

Why hadn't he pulled up his own log? Probably didn't even occur to him. Lucky guy.

Maybe if they talked about something they both knew well, that would take up all their attention. "Remember the year we joined the English peasants guild on a lark and they decided tae be the town militia?"

It worked. He rocked up and down with laughter. "Aye, I wull never forget it. I had tae teach ye tae fight with the quarterstaff. Ye were pretty good at it. Hae ye kept that up any?"

"Come on, when would I practice quarterstaff—"

The way he cut her off made her think he was deliberately steering the conversation away from the modern world, but she couldn't be sure. His eyes were lively and dazzling as ever, and she kept hers away from them as much as possible, lest she be caught and drawn in. "The funniest part o' that was when Conall said ye would never learn, sae Ashley made him teach her as wull!"

She couldn't help it, she burst out laughing too. "Was na that the best irony ever? If I dare say it myself, I was much better at it than she."

"Aye, ye were. Gabe had his work cut oot for him. Served him right." He rushed on to another subject, plainly not wishing her to ask after his twin. "But speaking o' not doing things wull, dae ye still hae the faire costume ye made? I will never forget how beautiful ye looked in it — nor Mither's face when she first saw it!" He slapped his knee, he was laughing at her so hard.

The kettle whistled, saving her from having to admit that yes, she did still have that costume. She had worked so hard on it. She still wore it on occasion.

She poured boiling water into both packages of lasagna, sealed them up, and set them down on the ground near their log, leaning against some rocks.

He reached for his.

She stopped his hand, then let go before he could hold her hand in return or even think it was like that between them. It wasn't. "It has tae sit a minute, or ye will na like it verra much." She got out the dried garlic bread and offered him his. "Here, we can eat this while we wait."

He took his, but he didn't open it. "Och, nay. Ye hae tae dip the garlic bread in the lasagna, ye ken."

They sat next to each other in amiable silence, willing the water to soak into the lasagna so they could enjoy it. She couldn't help but look over at him occasionally, and she saw how the fire now danced on his face in the twilight, making the angles of his cheekbones and jaw look especially masculine.

"One minute gone." He grabbed his packet of lasagna, tore it open, and stopped cold. "Ye hae any spoons?"

She snapped out of watching his muscular movements. "Och, aye." She dug around in the pack until she found extra-strong but feather-light plastic flatware —conveniently tucked into a flap that folded down, if she'd only studied the pack ahead of time to know where they were kept.

They munched quietly, watching the fire.

"Ye mentioned fruit punch?"

What was wrong with her? "Och, aye. Here." She opened the plastic bottle and drank a good half of the punch before handing it over. "Ye wull leave me none once ye taste it. 'Tis verra good, and my bet is ye have na had this in forever either."

He took the bottle and toasted her, then drank it all down in three gulps.

"I hear John defied your parents and stayed with Jaelle."

His face closed to her. "Then ye also heard he chickened oot at the last moment and did na marry her." He put a joking tone in his voice, but she could tell he meant what he said next. "Dinna tell him I said sae."

This was news. "John is here, in this time?"

He was scraping the last of his lasagna out of his packet with his remoistened garlic bread. "Aye, and syne we dinna want tae bring Kelsey in, he is oor best hope for finding Nadia and Ellie. Eoin is at Murray camp watching the boys. We wull see him tomorrow. O' course, he goes by Eoin in this time."

"I would hae stayed with ye, despite the family curse, if ye only had given me the chance tae." She looked over at him. She knew this was a taboo subject, but she had to try, and this seemed like the best chance she was going to get.

He had picked up his stir stick and was separating the coals so they would burn out quickly. He looked up at the sky and then over where Smoke munched grass near the creek. "It wull be dark soon. Dae ye want tae watch the last o' the coals, or wull ye go and get the blankets and lay them oot?"

"I wull watch the coals."

He balanced the fire stirrer on the ground and lowered his hand toward the middle of it so that her hand was nowhere near his when she took hold of the stick.

She used every bit of her willpower to watch the fire and not his magnificent kilted form as he walked over to Smoke and got the blanket. Stirring the coals was a good distraction. She was grateful for the opportunity to watch the embers glow when she blew on them to make them burn out faster. So many memories with Meehall at faire were swirling through her mind: all the set dances they did to the music of fiddle and bodhran. The play they had tried to do and failed miserably. Peeling potatoes for the guild's stew. So many starry nights like this one when they walked the empty fairgrounds together after hours, making plans for a future they were so sure they would share.

She shivered. Starry nights were beautiful, but they were cold. She used her fancy leather backpack as a pillow and got in, between the blankets, with Meehall.

"Yer teeth are chattering." He turned his back to her and pulled her up behind him as if they were once more on the horse. "Take my warmth. Ye need it."

And so, despite all her efforts, here she was. In bed with the man she wished loved her enough to make it work.

10

Meehall kissed Sarah again, soft and gentle to show her all the love he felt for her, all the joy she brought to his life.

She kissed him back with passionate devotion, the way she always had.

"I was meant tae be with ye," he told her breathlessly. "I feel it in my bones."

"As dae I," she responded, enthusiastically beginning another session of married bliss.

Hours later, when she lay peacefully sleeping in his arms, he ruminated. Why had his parents been so insistent that he leave her behind? It was working out fine. Birth control was a thing. There was nothing to worry about. They would have two kids and then stop.

In the morning, he put his arm around his wife and turned with her to look out the window of their modest cottage in the Highlands.

Inevitably, they turned and grinned at each other at how fun it had been to choose an old home that had been here for centuries. They could visit any time they wanted and still know the lay of the land.

She snuggled up closer to him, and he savored the warmth of her embrace as well as the sweet apple scent of her hair.

Nature called, spoiling the mood.

He pulled away from her to go take care of it — and woke up in Sarah's arms under the rising sun, with Smoke nickering beside the nearby stream.

This infatuation with Sarah was getting dangerous. He hadn't realized he was dreaming. It had seemed so real, and she had looked at him with such love in her eyes. He needed to watch himself.

When he got back to their nearly dead fire, Sarah was up.

Face washed and hair brushed, she was rummaging around inside that fascinating leather pack of hers. "I hae cold granola with dried milk for breakfast," she said when she saw him, trying to suppress her expectant smile.

He couldn't help but smile back in anticipation as he reached for the packet she held out "Dae ye aim tae spoil me for the rugged Scottish life tae which I hae grown accustomed?" He took his first bite, then closed his eyes in ecstasy as he chewed and tasted the grainy flavors he used to savor every morning, years ago. "Ye remember."

She smugly ate her own granola. "O' course I dae. I remember all sorts o' things ye did."

"Will it be sorry I am, for asking what?"

She winked. "Aye, could verra wull be ye will. Dae ye recall how ye could na be withoot yer phones, Gabe and ye?"

It was a fond memory, covertly texting with his twin. It really was. And all the more because Sarah shared it.

But he couldn't encourage her. His dream notwithstanding, he already had three sons. After Keith was born, he had tried using birth control with Cairstine. One could make rudimentary condoms out of animal intestines, and he'd done his best. It hadn't worked.

Something in Kelsey's changed mannerisms told him Druids had deliberately sabotaged his efforts to get even close to having a fourth son who would be obliged to serve them. At least he didn't have two sets of twins like his father.

No, he couldn't encourage Sarah's affections, and so he quit smiling at her in gratitude. Quit making appreciative eating noises. Quit paying attention to her altogether.

It was for her own good. He couldn't marry again. Three sons were enough. Plenty. He would consider himself done with women.

She wasn't stupid. He could tell right away she had figured out what he was doing. Several times she started to speak but then thought better of it and instead just concentrated on eating.

She had made another bottle of punch, but this time she didn't share it with him.

He didn't blame her.

It was a long way to Murray camp even on this their second day of travel. They took turns riding Smoke, the other walking by his side. They didn't need to stop much this way, only for water and the midday meal.

But when they came in sight of Murray camp, he realized he did need to tell her some things before they got there. "Straight away, I need tae meet with Eoin and my cousins, Ciaran and Baltair. I wull tell them what happened and see if Eoin he has any ideas on how we can find the Camerons and get the lasses back."

She kicked him from up on Smoke's back. Not hard, but her message was clear. "Eoin and I ken one another. There is na reason I canna gae with ye."

Staring straight ahead, he was firm with her. "Aye, there is. 'Tas been lang syne he saw ye. 'Twill be awkward between ye—"

"'Tis plenty awkward between me and ye."

"That is na the point."

"Wull what is the point?"

"We must needs get tae rescuing yer friends soon."

She grimaced at him, but she didn't argue anymore. "What wull I dae while ye are daeing that? I dinna ken anybody else in the camp."

"Eoin's wife Malina knows the secret. She wull be safe, and she can introduce ye around the camp."

"As yer wife?"

He took a deep breath and let it out in order to calm himself. "Aye, as my wife. That is best for both oor sakes. But Eoin, Malina, Ciaran, and Baltair wull ken the truth."

"What aboot yer sons?"

He swallowed. "Now that ye say that, having second thoughts, I am."

"Aboot time. I dinna want tae be introduced tae yer children as their new mother ainly for them tae believe I hae abandoned them when I gae haime."

"Aye."

"Sae who shall I be, then?"

"Eoin telt the Murrays he was marrit once afore. 'Twas the ainly story that made sense in 1700. Ye wull be a relative o' his first wife, the one who died. Ellie and Nadia will be in yer clan as wull."

"All right. Which clan am I in?"

"MacDrest."

"MacDrest?"

"Aye. Eoin made it up."

"Was that wise?"

"Nay one wull question it."

"How can ye be certain?"

"Nay one has, and Eoin has been here with the Murrays two years."

"That is na verra reassuring."

"There was a Drest, back in history, who had a son."

"How dae ye ken?"

"'Twas Eoin."

Wow. Sarah wrapped her mind around her

friend John from the faire starting a clan. "Verra wull."

It was easy to spot Malina's red hair before they reached the camp, and Meehall saw Alan, Keith, and Lyle chasing each other at the other end of Murray camp. It would be possible to speak with his brother before his sons made that difficult.

Good thing Eoin had shown Malina photos of everyone who might one day visit from the future. It had seemed a bad idea at the time, but Meehall saw now that his brother had been right to do it.

Malina's face went ashen for a moment when she first saw Sarah, but Eoin had married well. The hardy Scottish woman recovered quickly. "Meehall, who dae ye bring tae us?"

"Sarah MacDrest, this is Malina, wife o' Eoin, formerly the husband o' yer Mollie MacDrest. Malina, the news is na good. Two MacDrest lasses hae been captured by the Camerons. Here is hoping 'twill please ye tae introduce Sarah aroond while I go and hash this ower with Eoin."

Malina looked tentatively up at Sarah.

Meehall simply put Smoke's reins in Malina's hand and walked away before either lass could object.

"I need tae speak with Eoin," he told the first Murray he encountered. "Where is he?"

The man was busy slopping pigs, and he just hitched his thumb over his shoulder.

Meehall found and embraced his brother and cousins, but indicated the hill they had taken to climbing when they wanted to talk privately. Once they were far enough away, he told them all that had happened over the last few days.

"...And sae we looked all day, but there was na sign o' any footprint leaving the gathering area. The Cameron clan disappearit intae thin air, Eoin. How could they keep company with enough druids tae dae that withoot us hearing aboot it?"

Eoin flexed his bulging chest muscles. "'Tis nay more than one druid, Meehall. The Camerons hae a druid who can see and open the natural portals. These hae formerly been unheard o' in this time, but they were legendary in the time o' the Picts. 'Tis the only way I ken tae transport an entire clan at once. We need tae find the Camerons and take oot this druid, fast."

"Let us gae speak with the Murray."

11

S till atop Smoke, Sarah looked down and studied the beautiful redhead who Meehall's youngest brother had married — recently, if Eoin had first arrived in this time two years ago. From the way she studied Sarah in return, it was obvious Eoin's wife knew about time travel.

Malina's eyes searched all over Sarah. When she was done, disappointment showed on her face. And then she pinched the hem of Sarah's plaid Macbeth costume skirt. She turned it over and studied the stitches a few moments, smoothing them between her thumb and forefinger and going along a foot of fabric.

When Malina dropped the skirt, she looked both impressed and satisfied with herself. "Ye had best come doon. I am meant tae introduce ye aroond, and 'twill go better if ye are na riding. Ye canna get inside anyone's tent as ye are, nae can ye?"

Sarah held up her hand in a gesture of peace while pressing her lips together to show contrition. "O' course. Where shall I tie him up?"

Instead of answering her directly, Malina called out, "Rory!"

A red-headed boy who was almost a man and looked a lot like Malina appeared, running but not out of breath. "Mither?"

"Lyle?"

"Aye." Rory took the side strap of Smoke's bridle in his hand while looking up at Sarah, offering his hand.

She took it and had no sooner landed on her feet than Rory was up on Smoke, riding to where a bunch of other horses were tied.

Sarah watched him a moment, speaking to his mother out of the corner of her mouth. "I suppose Meehall just leaves everything in the saddlebags?"

"Aye." Malina looped her arm through Sarah's. It was a friendly gesture, and it surprised her. "Come, I will introduce ye tae the women o' Clan Murray."

Half an hour later, Sarah had heard 30 names she didn't think she was likely to remember, let alone associate with 30 faces. She looked to Malina to see if there would be a next stop.

Malina patted Sarah's hand in sympathy. "I suppose ye would like tae meet Meehall's sons, aye?"

Sarah's reaction to this surprised her. "Aye, I would."

Malina smiled and called out, "Alan, Keith, Lyle!"

Three boys came running, all looking like miniature variations of Meehall. From largest to smallest, their questions were:

"Who is this, Malina?"

"Where did she come from?"

"Is the bonny gaun'ae bide?"

After meeting Sarah's eyes to share a grin at Lyle's adorableness, Malina addressed Alan's question. "Lads, this is a friend o' yer da and his brother. Her name is Sarah."

"Hello, Sarah," Lyle said immediately.

Malina put a hand on Lyle's back and hugged him to her leg, gesturing first at one brother and then the other. "Sarah, this is Meehall's oldest, Alan. He is six and just lost his first tooth this morning. This is Keith, who is four, and Lyle, who is three."

Before Sarah could get a word in, the boys were pelting her with questions.

Keith tugged on her skirt. "How dae ye ken Da and Uncle?"

Lyle took her hand. "Are ye gaun'ae bide with us and be a Murray?"

In a low voice, Alan asked her, "Are ye a MacGregor tae?"

Keith asked, "Dae ye hae any sons we can play with?"

Lyle tugged on her hand until she looked at him. "Dae ye already hae a husband?"

Sarah pressed her lips together to stifle her laugh, but a chuckle came out despite her efforts. "I'm only here for a visit. Nay, I dinna hae a husband, and nay, I dinna hae any children."

Alan looked down, spun slowly around, then held his tooth up to his eyes to look at it some more.

But Lyle kept hold of Sarah's hand and sat down on some grass, pulling her down next to him. He looked her frankly in the eye. "Da has na been the same since Mither died. He needs a new wife."

Sarah looked at him just as seriously. "'Tis verra good o' ye, tae be looking oot for yer da."

Lyle puffed out his little chest and raised his chin.

Malina cleared her throat. "Speak o' the devil and he appears."

Sarah looked up from the charming young Lyle and saw Meehall about to join them, along with Eoin and two other men who must be their cousins. Seeing Meehall and his brother together brought bittersweet tears to her eyes, because the way they were walking conjured a memory of when they had walked up to her at the same distance from each other, in the same formation.

JAELLE'S HUGE SWORD WHOOSHED AT SARAH. Her face was red with pretend rage, and she yelled her usual relentless stream of overly honest conversation as a sort of battle cry, which could be heard by the cheering crowd sitting under red, green, and yellow-dyed burlap shaders in the stands. "Make peace with yer maker, for I am gaun'ae cut ye in twain! I hae been restful far tae lang!"

Without any theatrics of her own, Sarah whipped her quarterstaff around to bounce Jaelle's sword away with a satisfying thwack that made Jaelle bend down with its force, allowing Sarah to hold her long skirts up and back away five steps across the dirt arena. "Are ye certain we but play? Ye are making this verra realistic."

Jaelle rushed at Sarah again and struck from a different direction, making it more difficult for Sarah to parry. "Och, Sarah, ye can dae far better than this! Quit holding back! I can take it, ye ken. We hae tae make this look good, if we want tae hae a chance."

Sarah beat the sword away again, but only barely. "If we want to have a chance at what?"

Jaelle twisted her head and leaned over in an exaggerated motion that said Sarah's question had an obvious answer. "Your turn. Come at me. Make it convincing."

Sarah did. She ran at Jaelle with her quarterstaff whipping around to take advantage of its longer reach. "You may want a chance at being a fight instructor, but I sure don't."

Jaelle swung her hips back and moved her middle out of the way of Sarah's quarterstaff. "Why not?"

"The truth?" Sarah whirled around with a satisfying swirl of her skirts and hair —which she was disappointed that Meehall had to miss.

"'Bout over!" Called Peadar, Meehall's dad. "Clear the field."

This was the part Sarah didn't like. They had to go over to Peadar now and get critique on their fight. The critique wouldn't be so much about their technique as their theatricality. To her horror, she got good marks for theatricality but failed technique. Jaelle fared the opposite. The short answer was they wouldn't be instructors anytime soon.

Once they are safely away from him, Jaelle whispered, "Yes, the truth. Why do you keep taking stage fighting if you don't want a chance at instructor? You're plenty good enough for the shows already."

Sarah leaned in conspiratorially and whispered back to Jaelle, "I'm afraid that if I don't, I won't be included in everything, and I'll miss chances to be with Meehall."

Sarah usually hung out with Ashley at the faire, seeing how the two of them were dating twins. But for whatever reason, Meehall and Eoin had needed immunizations that day and gone to town to see the doctor, whereas the other girls' boyfriends hadn't. So they were sitting all cozy as couples with Dall and Emily's blessing — albeit the girls' parents didn't know. This was their carefully guarded secret, and they wondered how long they could keep it.

Jaelle was sulking. "It's just you and me, Sarah. Everyone else is doing something they like. Well, I suppose Meehall and Eoin are having a hard time."

"Are you kidding? They're having the time of their lives in town. I can't believe Vange let them drive by themselves. I'll be amazed if they make it to the doctor's office."

Jaelle smiled the tiniest bit through her sulk. "We should have gone with them."

Sarah smiled knowingly. "Next time, we will."

The two did their special handshake, sealing the deal, and then watched the rest of the bouts with a smug satisfaction they communicated with subtle looks. They were missing their guys.

Rapt on the sword fight in front of her, Sarah felt Jaelle nudge her side and looked up. She saw a scene very similar to the one which had brought this all up in her mind.

Meehall and Eoin walked toward her in the same formation, minus their two cousins. It was as if this were a predetermined way the two of them walked together.

The idea gave her shivers as she sat dazed, watching them approach in real life.

Sarah lowered her head so that Meehall wouldn't see the blush in her face at the memories of what happened later on that day.

They were walking under the stars like they always did when all the customers had gone home and it was only the faire people who spent the night here. This was the last night of the summer in North

America. Tomorrow, Meehall and Conall, Eoin and Jeff, Tavish and Tomas, and all of their parents would fly to Australia's spring and summer, along with the other key people from the faire.

Meehall would be gone until USA faire recruiting started in spring.

She looked up at his thoughtful face. "Text me every day. Promise."

He stopped and turned her to face him there under the stars in the field of recently mown hay. His kilt and long ash-blond hair flapped in the breeze. He had never looked so gorgeous. "Don't I always." It was a statement rather than a question, and he moved in to kiss her.

She kissed him back, but it was difficult with her tears turning into sobs. "I'm always afraid you'll meet someone down there, that you won't be interested in me anymore."

"Sarah, that will never happen. You're the one for me. We'll be married someday."

She clung to him, turning their romantic embrace into something she wasn't very proud of, but she couldn't bring herself to let go. She spoke against his chest through her sobs. "Promise? Promise I'm the one you're going to marry? And shouldn't you be asking me instead of telling me?"

He held her tenderly. "We're only 14, Sarah. I can't be asking you yet. But yes, I promise, both to text you and to marry you." He stroked her hair and caressed her back and did everything he always did when she was upset.

It worked, a bit. Her breathing slowed and she quit sobbing. The tears flowed down until she only needed to wipe them away every few breaths.

They held each other like that until it got too cold to stay outside anymore. And then they went to their separate tents, him to the boys' and her to the girls'.

🦢

MEEHALL SAT DOWN ON THE GRASS BESIDE Sarah and smiled at little Lyle's hand in hers. "'Tis all arranged. The Murrays ride tae find the Camerons on the morrow. I'm gang now tae take oor children and elderly tae stay with allies until the conflict is ower."

"Good," she told him, once more hopeful that Nadia and Ellie would soon be freed.

He put his hand over hers and Lyle's. "Let me take ye away as well. My mind will be more at ease if I ken ye are safe."

Lyle raised his head up proudly again. "I wull keep this bonny lass safe, Da."

Sarah gently squeezed Lyle's hand and addressed him, rather than Meehall. "I thank ye for the offer. Howsoever, I dae need tae ride with the Murrays. Some o' my friends hae been captured by the Camerons. I will na rest easy myself until I see them freed. If I stay behind, I will worry sae much that I will be terrible company for all o' ye."

"Verra wull," said Meehall. "Come, lads. We leave now."

They all ran off with their father.

Sarah was left with Malina, Eoin, and the cousins. She studied Eoin's face. He had changed. Way more than Meehall or even Kelsey had. Sarah wouldn't have recognized him from a distance, his muscles were so big.

Even as he sat there on the grass nearby, joking with his cousins, he was lifting a rock over and over, working his biceps. "Well met, Sarah. It has been a lang time. But Celtic University agrees with ye. Ye are the picture o' health."

"As are ye, Eoin. Look at ye!"

He flexed.

It made Sarah uncomfortable. She looked at

Malina while asking Eoin, "Are ye gaun'ae introduce me tae yer cousins?"

Malina shoved her husband playfully.

He grunted, never stopping his bodybuilding. "This here is Ciaran."

"Well met," she told the tall man with short dark hair.

"My pleasure."

Eoin shifted the rock to his other hand and worked his other biceps. "This fellow ower here is Baltair."

This other cousin was farther away and merely nodded.

Sarah nodded back, then turned to Eoin. "Tell me aboot these portals. Meehall says they were na used in the time o' Hadrian's Wall, but telt o' in many tales."

"Aye," Eoin said with a hint of a snarl. And every last one o' those tales ends badly, with those who dae na hae access tae the portals dying horrible deaths. I dae na ken enough tae be helpful, but I ken someone who will be. When my brother returns, we must pay him a visit."

❧ 12 ❧

Meehall whistled on his way over to the single lasses's tent to get Sarah. He had slept like a baby last night, thanks to his relief at not having her next to him. Having her so close was anything but relaxing.

She must've been waiting for him, because she rushed out as soon as he arrived. "I'm all ready tae gae." She was bright eyed and bushy tailed, just like him.

Seeing her so eager raised his spirits. "Verra good," he told her sincerely as he led her over where the horses were tethered.

She gave him a curious look when he walked right by Smoke.

He returned it with one of cautious generosity

when he stopped by a white mare with a quarterstaff strapped to her side. "Snow's saddlebags are laden with provisions for ye. Maisie's son made certain o' that last evening before we slept. Dae ye need help getting on?" He stirruped his fingers to give her a boost.

"I dinna, but I wull take it. Thanks!" She was up straddling Snow's back in no time, giving him a knowing look and settling herself over the quarterstaff and the rug that softened it a bit. "Oh, she's still tied up. Will ye dae the honors?"

"Aye." He untied Snow, but instead of giving Sarah the reins just yet, he led the mare over next to smoke and mounted first. "I dinna ken how long it has been syne ye rode alone. 'Tis glad I am ye took lessons, but we canna take tae much care, ye ken."

She must've slept exceptionally well, because she was all jiggly with excitement and pent-up energy. And that made her more attractive than anything. Even when she rolled her eyes at him for some reason. "Och, I dae well enough. Lead the way."

He chuckled, then leaned his head over where everyone was gathering for the journey. "Ye may be better at riding than afore, but yer sense o' observation has na improved, I see."

She smacked him on the upper arm with the

back of her hand and ran Snow over to join the others, stopping neatly when she arrived next to Malina, Rory, and Eoin. Immediately, she started chatting with Malina.

But Meehall saw the look on Eoin's face, and it was not approving. He had better get over there fast before sparks flew between his brother and their mutual friend. What had gotten into his youngest brother?

Yep, they had been bickering. Sarah was looking pointedly away from Eoin when Meehall arrived on Smoke.

"Come on, Sarah. I want tae hae a word with Ciaran and Baltair."

Relief took over her face as she followed him down the party a ways. It was a good-sized party, three dozen warriors, all riding single. They would make good time, once they figured out where the Camerons were.

Meehall's cousins smiled at Sarah, and to give them credit, they didn't stare too much. Knowing there were male time travelers was one thing, but apparently female time travelers were fascinating. He'd heard them speak of nothing else since she arrived —except for her female time traveler friends.

The ride over the mountain was uneventful, but

Eoin sneered at Sarah while discussing their plans to free Nadia and Ellie. Ciaran and Baltair were kind to Sarah, though, and Meehall was glad he could take her away from Eoin and enjoy their company sometimes.

His brother was leading the party to a sacred grove, and talk of it reminded Meehall —and everyone else— of Cairstine. His clan were sharing memories of his late wife whenever they thought he couldn't hear. His own memories threatened to swamp him into grief anew, just when he thought he was doing better.

When they got to flat land again, Sarah took off on Snow. She passed by before Meehall was able to shake off his glum mood and catch up with her.

"Race me to that first tree of the woods!" she exulted.

This would be easy. He kicked Smoke into a run.

The race was on. They rushed through the heather, jumping over a few small streams and rocks on their way. It was amazing how good Sarah had gotten at horse riding. He beat her to the tree, but only barely.

And then he made the mistake of meeting her eyes.

The way her face was flushed with excitement did him in. He rode right up to her side and gazed into her eyes. Seeing in them everything he was looking for, he leaned in, eager to taste her lips on his. Anticipating the way she would respond wholeheartedly. Not thinking about the consequences, the family curse, or anything beyond this moment. This perfect moment.

He was close to her lips. He could feel her breath on his cheeks. And then there was a rustling of the grass behind him, and the horses stamped a bit apart. The perfect moment was ruined.

Meehall turned Smoke in anger to face whoever had done this and give that person a piece of his mind. Seeing it was his brother only steeled his resolve. He might have known. The bodybuilder was taking his role as leader to the sacred grove entirely too seriously. "What the hell, Eoin?"

His brother sat up tall on Fire and made two loose claw fists at him and Sarah. "Ye dinna need tae be racing! This is a serious expedition, and ye two are taking it lightly. I wull hae tae separate ye for the rest o' the—"

Meehall's reflexes kicked in, making Smoke rear up on his hind legs and tromp the air with his forelegs.

Eoin backed down, but his fists were still brandished.

From up on the rearing horse, Meehall pointed at his little brother. "Ye wull dae na such thing!"

Eoin stood his ground now.

Meehall didn't want to hurt his brother, so he gave Smoke the signal to bring his front down. "Ye ken why. 'Tis safest if she remains with us, including Ciaran and Baltair. But she canna ride alone with them."

Eoin snickered. "Ye fear they wull steal her from ye."

Meehall wasn't going to give his brother the satisfaction of a rise. Instead, he forced himself to chuckle. He had learned long ago that the best way to avoid confrontation with his brother was to take his sayings as jokes. "Aye, indeed there is that. Canna hae them getting too serious aboot her." He met Sarah's eyes then, intending to let her know it was a jest.

But her reaction floored him. She was still staring at him adoringly, just as she had been when he was about to kiss her.

Eoin moved in between them, denying them the privacy to discuss it. "If ye insist on being together, then ride with me and help me lead. Ye can invite oor cousins up there with us if you like, but ye wull be staying with me where I can keep an eye on ye. Nay more frivolity. I mean it. We are almost tae the sacred grove where I can summon the auld druid one time. Once I dae, we had better get all the answers we need, because like I said, I can only summon him one time." He looked at Sarah directly. "I'm using this one chance on yer friends, ye ken."

They had ridden up to the front and joined Malina and Rory. Malina saw what was happening between Eoin and Sarah and rode out to meet them. Falling in next to Sarah, she addressed her husband. "Frivolity adds a bit o' fun now and again, if I recall correctly."

Sarah smiled at Malina in thanks before she turned back to Eoin. "I agree. Nay more faffing aboot. I thank ye for using yer one chance at the druid tae help my friends." She held out her hand in the modern way, for a shake.

Eoin looked at it, then up into her eyes, and raised his brows. At least he was no longer yelling.

Catching herself in the anachronism, Sarah lowered her hand and nodded matter-of-factly at Eoin. And then she froze and whispered to Meehall, "If we canna trust Kelsey, what makes Eoin think we can trust this ancient druid he can summon?" Her whisper was soft enough that only their family could hear.

Meehall met his brother's eye and raised his brows.

Eoin moved his hand in a smoothing motion in front of him.

Meehall turned back to Sarah. "I asked the verra same question myself last night. But Eoin says he trusts this Deoord. Besides, I dinna see any other options."

Ciaran and Baltair did ride up and join them as they got underway once more with the whole company of warriors. Sarah rode next to Meehall and Malina rode beside her husband. Eoin spoke frequently to Meehall over his shoulder.

They had left the meadow and were riding through forest again when Sarah dropped the bomb.

"Tell me about Cairstine."

No one had spoken directly to him about his late wife since her death except his sons.

Instantly, a painful sob racked Meehall's throat.

He choked it down. Sarah needed to realize how in love he had been with Cairstine. How much she had meant to him. "She was popular among the Murray clan. She knew all the old stories and would tell them around the fire. She taught them tae the boys as best she could. Alan remembers a few, and betimes, I can coax him tae sit still long enough tae tell one. She tried tae teach me, but I dinna hae the memory for it."

He choked up again, frustrated that he couldn't even pass on this part of his wife's legacy.

Sarah gave him a sympathetic pat on the forearm and then drifted away from him again to ride around the other side of a tree, quietly muttering "Bread and butter" while waiting for him to resume his tale.

He did. "She was sae good with the children, always talking tae them and singing. 'Twas na only oor children, either. All the wee ones o' the clan loved her. There hae been schools in Scotland for ten years nae, but we canna stay in one place lang enough tae hae continuity o' lessons. Cairstine taught them, Sarah. The children o' his clan can read!"

"Wow!" Sarah said in English before she caught herself and switched back to Gaelic. "Sounds like she was an amazing woman."

Meehall took a deep breath against the grief that threatened to crush his chest "Even that isna all. She was devoted tae me as well, defending me. Anyone who had a word tae say against me was in one o' her stories the next day. She didna kill them off, but she did cast them as the villains. There was much debate among the clan whether she was doing this on purpose, but elders who knew the real names in the stories assured me that aye, my wife was defending me."

Sarah started to give him another sympathy pat, but at the last moment she pulled back, instead just riding next to him quietly as their horses minced the spaces between the tree roots of the forest.

"Cairstine rode tae battle with me. She didna fancy the fighting, didna hae any talent for it, but she made me teach her sword sae she could help, blessed lass. She did learn passing well. Nay sae well as ye did learn the quarterstaff, mind, but well enough. She was as devoted a wife as a man could want, and I miss her dearly, sae verra dearly."

She left him alone so far as talk went, but she stayed by his side and kept him company, giving Eoin a stern look when he started to approach them and actually turning him away.

"I thank ye for that, but we dae need tae hear what my brother has tae say. Nay maire questions aboot Cairstine. I dinna want tae speak o' her ever again, ye ken?"

"Aye," was all she said as the two of them rode back up to the front with Meehall's kin.

"About time," Eoin said as he turned to look down the half mountain into the forest that rested below. "Dae ye see in the center where the tallest oak and rowan trees grow?"

"Aye," everyone said.

"'Tis a sacred grove. There, one time ainly, I can speak with that ancient druid I ken."

Sarah tied Snow up with the other horses and followed Meehall, Eoin, Ciaran, and Baltair into the thicker part of the oak and rowan forest. "Is na Malina tae come with us?" she asked Eoin's back.

He didn't answer, just kept climbing over twisted branches.

Meehall leaned down to whisper near her ear, "Eoin forbade her tae come tae the sacred grove. Says 'tis tae fraught with danger. She wanted tae accompany him anyhow, and he had tae appeal tae her that Rory might na be left with ainly one parent." His breath tickled, and yet she didn't flinch away.

Wanting to feel more of his breath but knowing that wouldn't be wise, Sarah sighed, instead beginning to tread over the gnarled roots of huge old oaks and rowan trees. "It has na improved his mood at all."

"Nay, it has na."

"Dae ye believe this grove is a danger tae us?"

THE MURRAYS HAD SURROUNDED THE SACRED grove to guard them lest intruders appear.

Eoin was leading, as usual. "The rest o' ye are along tae guard me. I wull speak with Deoord."

It wasn't really a question, so no one answered him.

Sarah hid the tiniest smile at Eoin's expense. He probably took their silence for agreement, when it was far from that. She looked over to see if Meehall shared her amusement.

He didn't. His face showed only hope and reassurance. "Have na fear, Sarah. Soon, yer friends wull be free."

Sobered, she forced a smile. "I thank ye again for coming with me on this quest. I feel sae foolish for jumping at the chance tae time travel."

He pulled some bushes back to help her go through the forest. "Dinna be sae hard on yerself."

She went through and then moved aside again,

so that they were walking close, but not touching. "What sort o' friend am I, tae lead them intae captivity?"

Surprising her, Ciaran spoke up. "Ye are the kind o' friend who goes after them and seeks their release. Who does na give up. Ye are the type o' friend good tae hae."

Surprised and taken off guard, Sarah mumbled, "I thank ye. I dinna feel that way at all."

Ciaran rushed toward the next bush, reaching out his hand toward some branches which blocked the trail. "Well that is the kind o' friend ye are, and ye need tae ken."

Meehall rushed ahead and pulled aside the branches, beating Ciaran there by a millisecond. "Aye, Nadia and Ellie are fortunate tae hae ye as a friend."

From up ahead, Eoin's voice came booming out. "Cut that silly banter oot, all o' ye, and come ower here intae the sacred grove and guard me, already. While ye hae been caterwauling, I hae made all the preparations. Ye are holding up this expedition."

Sarah made her way through the remaining smaller trees into the small grove of large oaks and rowans. Maybe it was her imagination, but it seemed like the trees were dancing ever so slowly in a circle around a flat boulder that loomed in their midst.

Eoin was seated atop the flat boulder. In his hand was a tiny vial with a silver stopper. "Years ago, Deoord promised tae heed my summons if I poured out this vial inside a sacred grove." Flexing all his muscles, he looked up and addressed the trees, a solemn and self-important look on his face. "I dae this for the Murrays and MacGregors at the expense o' the Camerons. I summon ye, Deoord, tae tell us how tae defeat the Camerons. Tell us how 'tis they travel such distances withoot dozens o' druids in their midst. Give us aid tae find them and defeat them." He poured a thick black liquid out of the tiny vial onto the stone.

The liquid ate at the stone, making acrid smoke rise up.

Sarah didn't want to feed Eoin's self importance by watching, but she couldn't help it. And then she had other things to think about.

The smoke over the hole being eaten in the stone shimmered. Colors swirled around. It was a meaningless swirl at first, but soon it all came together into the likeness of a very old man with wrinkled skin and gnarled hands. He was wearing a white linen robe that had seen much wear, judging by the stains on it.

Oddly, the stains didn't make the robe look used but rather, seasoned. The man's hair was long and silver. And on his head was a crown of mistletoe. His pale eyes were open, but they plainly did not see, being unfocused and devoid of recognition.

The druid spoke in a voice that belonged to a much younger man, sturdy and sure. "Yer need must be great, Eoin. As 'twas agreed, this wull be the one and ainly time I come tae ye."

Eoin didn't waste any time with pleasantries. "Where has the Cameron clan gone with the lasses, Deoord? Which is our fastest route tae them? How can we get the lasses away with the least amount o' bloodshed on oor side? Tell me!"

Deoord didn't cower at Eoin's angry words, but he wasn't quick to answer, either.

Spittle flew out of Eoin's mouth. His face became red and his hands once more clawed into fists, which he shook at Deoord. "Tell me! That acid will eat through the stone before your slow voice responds!" Meehall's brother lunged forward as if to shake the old Druid, but his hands went right through the apparition, which was gone for a moment with a break in the smoke before re-congealing into the likeness of Deoord.

Sarah couldn't stand it. She'd heard of this

happening before, with overeager students at Celtic University. Druids didn't like being dictated to, and they would do everything in their power not to satisfy demands.

She addressed the Druid in the way of the university's hired secretarial staff. "Please. Please tell me where my friends are and how I can save them."

The slightest smile took to the face of the old druid even as Eoin kept ranting and raving at him.

Deoord addressed his answer to Sarah, with his unseeing eyes. "The Cameron clan does hae a druid child." He left it at that, pausing as if waiting for her to exclaim. When she didn't, he went on. "Sculpted from dirt and created from magic, druid children hae nay parents. The earth is their mother. They see openings in space, openings that exist naturally and have since the beginning of time. Druid children are rare, and verra powerful. The Cameron clan's druid child has na found portals for time travel yet, only portals that travel distance in the blink of an eye. But once she discovers how tae find portals that gae agin time, the Murray clan is doomed." He started to fade away.

Desperate at the idea that he would be gone and she wouldn't know how to save her friends, Sarah sobbed with grief, letting out her heart's desire in a whisper, begging the old Druid to help her. "How dae I find my friends? The Camerons have captured them!"

Just before he faded away, Deoord looked right at her. "Find them soon, verra soon. The Cameron clan has some aught planned for them. An abomination agin this waurld. Gae west. 'Tis na far. And dinna lose heart. The druid child can ainly travel through portals. There are na portals near the sacred groves."

"A thousand times, I thank ye!" Sarah said through tears of relief. She was puzzled about the portals and the sacred grove. Why had he said that? But he was fading again, and she had a much more urgent question. "Och, and I beg o' ye, afore ye leave us, pray dae tell how Jaelle fares?"

On hearing Jaelle's name, Deoord's features softened. He quit fading. "Jaelle is a blessing tae my people, and I dinna mean ainly as the wife o' my clan chieftain and mither o' his bairns. She is o' prime import tae us as a fighting teacher. Her training in the ways people fight in the future hae gained us the upper hand in the region. We are safe on account o' her expertise."

This made Sarah smile even though her tears still

flowed. "Jaelle did in all ways wish tae be a fighting teacher."

Deoord drifted to her on the breeze, and when he put his ethereal hand on her cheek, Sarah thought for a moment she actually felt contact. "I can see that ye miss yer friend and regret the loss o' her company. Yer loss is oor gain. I ken 'twas na yer choice, but I thank ye for the sacrifice nonetheless. We are verra glad she came tae oor time."

Sarah might have imagined it, but Deoord looked over at Eoin in disapproval before he was gone.

They were ten steps away from the grove when Sarah heard her name and looked back to see the ancient druid had returned.

"Dinna fash ower much," he called out to her. "The portals dinna open tae the sacred groves, but always several hoors ride, sae nay one can surprise us there."

She shared a confused look with Meehall, and then the Druid faded away for good.

❧ 14 ❧

Meehall rushed to keep up with his brother, hurdling over roots and kicking acorns on his way out to the perimeter of the sacred grove. He couldn't see them through the thick trees, but he knew the Murray clan's warriors stood guard out beyond them. Without a care who heard, he shouted, "Eoin, wait for the rest o' us. Ye dinna want tae leave us, dae ye? We wull hae yer back in a fight afore any o' the Murrays dae!"

Even as he said this, Meehall knew his brother did wish to leave the Murrays behind. The druids sent Eoin on errands, which because of the MacGregor curse, Eoin couldn't refuse. The Murrays couldn't know about the errands or the curse anymore than they could be allowed to find out about time travel, or there would be hell to pay from the druids.

The first Murray Eoin encountered was one of the men usually sent to scout, young and light on his huge bay gelding. "Bran, quick, gather the other scouts and fly. The Cameron clan is camped west o' here. We hae tae find them. Gae!"

Bran was running off to find the other scouts when he ran right into Searc, the Murray clan chieftain, who stopped him. "Nay sae fast," Searc said as if to Bran, but he was looking right at Eoin. "I would hear all that went on with the druid ye summoned."

Meehall had caught up now, and he approached Searc. "'Tis true. The Druid did say the Cameron clan lies west o' here, and na far. He bade us make haste, says an abomination be planned for Sarah's clanswomen."

Meehall admired Searc's calmness and level head. The clan chieftain looked to where Sarah, Ciaran, and Baltair were just now coming out of the trees. "Baltair, what transpired in there? Did an auld Druid appear, indeed? What did the man say?"

Eoin leaned in. "We already telt ye what he did say. As well he said we must needs make haste—"

Searc turned on Eoin, and Searc's hackles were

up: spine rigidly straight, shoulders back, consider-able muscles bulging. When the chieftain spoke, it was with the strength of power realized, rather than the yearning of power sought. "I thank ye, Eoin, for doing what ye could tae find the answers we seek. I wull now decide what is tae be done, ye ken?"

Eoin opened his big fat mouth to protest and get himself shunned by the whole Murray clan, if not Meehall, Ciaran, Baltair —and Sarah and Malina as well.

Meehall put out a hand on his little brother's arm and pulled him away from Searc.

Eoin turned on Meehall with a fist ready to strike his nose.

But Malina was there now, and she stepped in front of Meehall just in time. "Eoin, Searc is the clan chieftain."

Eoin seemed on the verge of objecting again, but looking into his wife's eyes, he slowed his breathing. His mouth closed from a grimace, and he slowly lowered his fist to his side. "Aye, o' course Searc is the clan chieftain, and we await his decision on what should be done."

Searc had turned his back on Eoin the moment Meehall pulled him away. The chieftain was facing Baltair, who was giving his own recollection of what happened. Which was the same as Meehall's and Eoin's.

Apparently satisfied, Searc looked up into the setting sun. "We make camp just west o' here. Bran, rally the scouts and gae west. Find the Camerons and return."

⁂

MEEHALL DIDN'T NOTICE IT AMID THE HUBBUB of setting up camp, but once they were seated around the family fire, he saw the worry, sadness, and down-right despair in Sarah's eyes. Feeling guilty for ignoring his friend's distress, he reached out and gathered her up against him in a hug as they sat there side-by-side in the dirt by the fire. For a moment, he merely held her as they watched the flames rise against the darkness outside their wee family's circle of light.

But in a minute she was sobbing out her tale of woe as she clung to him and her tears wet his shoul-der. "Nadia and Ellie are wonderful friends, Meehall, as wonderful as ye and Jaelle and how Eoin used tae be. We were all such wonderful friends, remember?"

"Aye, I remember." He ran his hand in small circles on her back, in an attempt to calm her.

She kept sobbing. "Nadia went oot o' her way tae make me feel at home when I first came tae Celtic University. She is the one who invited me tae lunch that first time and said tae come back every day after. I ken the three o' us are the ainly American clarks at Celtic, but she didna hae tae dae that. She makes me feel like we hae been friends forever." She struggled against her sobs. "And Ellie. Ellie is sae much fun, sae full o' wonder. But she has been hurt in her past, Meehall. She tries tae hide it by jesting all the time, but ye can see it if ye pay her heed. 'Tis a crime that I let such a person fall intae such a dreadful situation."

"Wheesht." Meehall kept trying.

But she clutched him in obvious agony, sobbing and going on. "How could I be sae stupid as tae bring such peace-loving women tae this feud-driven time? They are such angels, sae selfless and good. They dinna deserve what I hae brought them tae! They could be safe in the hallowed walls o' the school, writing and smiling and pressing flowers, but I hae dragged them intae a hell! Their bonnie faces wull be drawn in horror ere long!"

As he continued trying to mollify Sarah, Meehall noticed something.

Ciaran and Baltair were sitting around the fire, too, but they weren't talking, not even in respectful hushed tones, like Eoin and Malina were. They were careful not to look at him and Sarah, but it was obvious to Meehall that his distant MacGregor cousins were listening intently to Sarah's portrayal of the other two modern women.

Meehall didn't get the chance to soothe Sarah into calmness.

Eoin jumped up when Searc was passing by their fire. "If 'tis true the scouts hae found the Camerons, then now is the time tae attack. While we can surprise them. Afore we are spotted!"

Meehall deliberated for just a moment. On the one hand, he had a friend who needed comforting. On the other hand, his stupid brother was going to get himself killed by the clan chieftain. It was a close call, but he chose his brother, jumping up and jogging over. "Eoin, let Searc make a plan—"

Eoin rounded on Meehall. This time, he did slug him. He kept slugging, making Meehall duck about. "Had yer wheesht! Ye are a coward, Meehall. A coward who would rather sit aboot the fire with the auld folks, blubbering about how bad the waurld is. This calls for the action o' warriors, na the blubbering o' cowards. Stay behind. Let the warriors attack. Now. This verra night."

Meehall wasn't going to take this from his younger brother, no matter how big Eoin had gotten. He ran at his brother and tackled him.

The two of them rolled around in the dirt of the pathway through the camp, all jabbing elbows and snapping teeth, like two small boys.

Meanwhile, Searc rallied the clan. "Warriors! We ride this verra night. Past the inn and clear up the mountain afore we sleep. At first light, we attack."

❧ 15 ❧

In the earliest light of the morning, Sarah and Snow reluctantly stopped to let Meehall and Smoke go on without them. Meehall was to follow Eoin, Ciaran, Baltair, and the Murray warriors down the last hill of the mountain to attack the Cameron camp. Sarah was to stay put in the relative safety of the trees that ended here.

Putting on a brave, grateful face and letting Snow prance about a bit for the show of reining her in again, Sarah told Meehall, "Dinna waste any time at heroics, ye ken. Just get my friends and come back. Ye dinna hae tae take oot my revenge for me."

Meehall drew the back of his hand across his forehead in exaggerated theatrics. "Whew! That is such a relief. I thank ye."

Sarah shared a smile with one of her oldest faire friends, a smile born of the love of acting.

And then without further ceremony, he turned and rode off at a gallop to catch up with the others, long hair and kilt both billowing in the wind.

She watched him and all the other warriors ride with mixed feelings. They had to rescue Nadia and Ellie, simply had to, but Meehall might be hurt, or even killed. Sarah wasn't selfish enough to tell him not to go, to put his life up as more important than the lives of her girlfriends. Never. But the idea of losing him tore at her heart in a way it hadn't the first time he rode off to rescue them.

She knew her mistake. She had let herself get attached to Meehall again, woe be to her. How had she let that happen in the span of just a few days? More importantly, how was she to undo it in less time than the years it had taken before?

"Hell mend ye, Sarah. Ye did bring this upon yerself. Ye kenned 'twas his bracer and he would want it back. Ye poked the boar, now take its wrath."

The Murrays reached the camp, and even from her distance up the hill, Sarah could hear swords ringing against each other in battle. They hadn't caught the Camerons off guard. Of course not. They were Highlanders too. They had set watches. But it appeared to be going in the Murray favor.

Sarah made herself take regular breaths. It wouldn't be over soon enough.

Straining her eyes to see in the distance any sign of Nadia and Ellie, she froze. Amid the fighting — and apparently unnoticed by anyone else— stood a woman in a white hooded robe. This woman was chanting, but the words were indistinct at this distance.

As if the druidess were invisible to everyone but Sarah, the warriors clashed swords behind her, but she remained not only untouched, but unregarded.

Certain it was what she must do, Sarah urged her white horse slowly forward into the thigh-high grass beyond the cover of the trees. She needed a better look at this female druid. Had to see what that face looked like. Had to hear which words she was uttering. It was important.

The everpresent Scottish cloud cover grew thicker, further dimming the feeble light of the sun.

A tiny voice in the back of Sarah's mind objected. 'This is na yer duty. Ye are meant tae stay behind, where 'tis safe.'

'Why should I, when clearly I must investigate?

Ainly I can. The warriors dinna hae a clue o' this druidess's presence.'

'There be a reason,' her mind insisted, 'a good one.'

'Wull then, what is it?'

'Uh... wull... Ye see... '

'Ye are na verra convincing. I just need tae be a mite closer tae the lass. I hae tae ken what she says. Simply hae tae ken.'

At first, Snow willingly carried Sarah around rock and tree toward the white-robed chanting woman. But about three quarters of the way down the hill, the horse braced against going forward.

Annoyed, Sarah kicked the horse's sides. "Yah! Yah, Girl!"

Nothing. Well, the horse's tail whipped up and slapped Sarah's back with a sting. Pesky flies.

Sarah leaned all the way forward and squeezed with her lower legs. "Yah!"

This time, the tail hit Sarah's butt with a fwap.

There was nothing for it. Sarah got down off the horse. Her foot caught on the quarterstaff tied there. She wrench the staff free to get it out of the way and then figured she might as well carry the staff. Absent-mindedly, she twirled it around herself like the broom she practiced with at Celtic as she walked toward the druidess.

Snow blew air out her nose, stomped, and munched grass, flapping her tail about all the while.

Whatever. Just a little closer, and Sarah would be able to see the woman's face, discern the words of her chant.

Sarah was running down the hill now.

'Run from boulder to boulder, and hide!' urged that pesky voice in the back of Sarah's mind.

But Sarah ran as fast as she could these last few yards. Any second now, any moment, she would see, would hear. Would know what she desperately desired to know. Ah!

Up close, the woman's face was ageless, but that of a mother. It was kindly and beckoning, and the woman's voice! Comforting was the best word for it—

Out of nowhere, Sarah felt acute pain in her left arm, making her yell, "Ouch!" and turn quickly to see what had happened. She felt her quarterstaff make hard contact with something as she turned and heard a grunt and the sound of a body hitting the ground.

Pain!

Oh, how her arm hurt!

Sarah looked around, puzzled. Apparently, the

pain brought with it a loss of memory somehow. What the heck was she doing out here in the middle of the battlefield? How had she gotten here? She couldn't indulge her puzzlement, though.

A sword came at her, and she assumed it had been what hurt her arm.

She thwacked the sword away with her quarterstaff, but her arm was growing weak, and come to think of it, so was she, in general.

"Fer the luv o' God, Sarah! Ye agreed tae stay away from the battle!" Meehall rode up from behind her attacker and took him out.

Spots danced in the air before Sarah's eyes, and her knees buckled.

Meehall rode Smoke over to break her fall.

She passed out.

Sarah woke up in front of Meehall on Smoke's back. Anxious, she turned —and was relieved to see Snow being led behind them. "Ye hae the right o' it. I should hae practiced more with my quarterstaff. But the druids at Celtic frown on their clerks training with weapons."

When he didn't say anything, she set her sails for

a different tack. "I thank ye for catching me. Where is it we gae? Is na the battle still on, back there?"

He tensed up the slightest bit, behind her. "Aye, it is, but ye need a safe place tae rest, and tae heal from that wound. What were ye doing anyway, Sarah? Ye promised tae stay behind."

She tried to answer, but again she saw spots.

This time, he pulled her back against him as she slumped into blackness.

SARAH WAS MUCH MORE COMFORTABLE WHEN next she woke, in a bed with a roof over her head. But she grabbed Meehall's hand as he moved to put it on her forehead. "We canna hae returned tae Inverness already, can we? I canna hae been oot that long, and ye canna hae ridden us that far away from Nadia and Ellie. Tell me ye did na."

He took her temperature with his other hand and seemed convinced she wasn't feverish. "Nay, we hae na returned tae Inverness. Ye wull recall we passed an inn on oor way tae Cameron camp last night, at the top oo the mountain. 'Tis where we are nae. Ye are safe enough. The Murrays were winning the battle, when we left."

She tried to get up, but her arm stung something awful, and besides, she felt woozy. Why... Oh yeah. "I must hae lost sae much blood, as I am utterly spent."

"'Twill all be right." He got up and moved toward the door. "Ye are settled nae, sae if ye wull excuse me—"

She tried to get up again, desperate not to be left behind. "Nay, dinna leave me."

He hung his head dramatically. "'Twill na be for long. I just gae doon tae the kitchen tae get ye some tea. Tae help ye sleep."

More like he needed to go back and help his fellow clan members in the battle. She shouldn't hold it against him. He'd done too much for her already. He was right, she was safe here. Best to be gracious about it. "Verra wull. I thank ye for bringing me here, Meehall. On with ye." She even made a shooing gesture.

"Right back," he told her as he turned around and closed the door.

She heard him walk down the stairs. Well, at least she wasn't entirely helpless. She had the bracer in her bag and she could use it to go back to the 21st Century, if worse came to worst and he didn't come back.

Get a grip on yourself, Sarah.

Fortunately, her backpack was in reach. She fished out some antiseptic ointment and dabbed it all over her wound, then bandaged it up as best she could with one hand.

But wonder of wonders, she'd no sooner done that than the door opened and Meehall came in with a cup of tea. He set it down on the nightstand, sat on the bed, tenderly helped her sit up, then picked up the tea and held it near her mouth. "Here, ye need tae drink this sae ye can sleep and heal."

With butterflies in her stomach at how tender he was being, Sarah made herself stop and think. Was it a sleeping tea as he had promised?

But this was Meehall. Sure, he had left her without so much as a goodbye all those years ago, but he had never hurt her. He had saved her life today.

She took the tea. "I thank ye." She drank it down all at once. "I thank ye verra much."

He looked at the bandage on her arm and over to her bag. "I see ye hae been busy."

"Aye, antiseptic ointment for the win."

He laughed a little. "Good. I'm glad ye had that. Unheard o' in these times, ye ken."

Feeling a little slap happy, she joined in. "Ye dinna say?"

He smiled at her tenderly, making her feel all warm and fuzzy inside.

But the effects of the tea were surprisingly fast, it having been drunk on an empty stomach, and before long at all, a deep black sleep enveloped Sarah.

❧ 16 ❧

Meehall waited until Sarah's breathing was regular so that he knew she was asleep, and then he rifled through her backpack. There had to be a medkit in here. She had everything else. Ah, he found it. And good, there was a sterile needle and thread, along with a local anesthetic.

If he didn't stitch her wound closed, it would scar, and she would hate that. Oh, any warrior would wear a scar with pride, but Sarah was not really a warrior. In her heart, she was a sage, the type of person others took their troubles to.

He knew that way back when, she'd only taken up the quarterstaff to impress him. He had been more selfish then, and he had let her. Theatrically, she was good at quarterstaff, with all the twirling she did. But she was not a skilled fighter when it came down to actual battle. She had swung at thin air today, when there was a warrior coming at her.

Why had he let her come along to the battle? He should have insisted she stay here at the inn, if not back at the safe haven with the children and elders.

He peeled the bandage off her arm. Good thing she had that antiseptic ointment. She'd rubbed off the scab and rubbed the ointment into the wound very well and thoroughly. It was a gaping wound, 3 inches long.

He set to work stitching it up neatly. It was an exacting task that took him a while. He had done this before several times for many friends and relatives, so it shouldn't have been affecting him the way it was, but affect him, it did. Before this moment, he hadn't realized how deeply he still cared for Sarah.

After he finished stitching, Meehall surprised himself by getting sleepy as well. He got on the other bed and fell fast asleep.

❧

MEEHALL WAS AWAKENED BY EOIN'S ECSTATIC

voice. "We won the battle. We won! Dae ye hear me, Meehall? We won! 'Tis a happy day. Wake up, wake up!"

Meehall sat up and rubbed his eyes, then looked quickly over at Sarah. She wasn't even roused by the yelling, so only a few hours had passed and she was still under the power of the tea.

Meehall looked to his brother. "Good. Good, sae where are Nadia and Ellie?"

Eoin's face didn't fall. No, he merely looked annoyed, not even disappointed, just annoyed. "Half the Camerons managed tae escape us through a portal that closed when we and the Murrays approachit. They took the lasses with them. Howsoever, we dae hae a lead, a captive we found alive on the battle-field. I hae volunteered tae interrogate him." He rushed out and could be heard taking the stairs two at a time.

What? Meehall couldn't let his little brother interrogate someone. He jumped up and rushed downstairs, then outside, where he saw his brother huddled next to a man who was sitting on the ground and tied with his back to a stake. He went to pull Eoin away from the man and talk some sense into his brother.

But Searc, clan chieftain of the Murrays, gestured.

Two men ran over and held Meehall by the arms, keeping him from interfering in the interrogation while Searc asked question after question.

Meehall relaxed in their grip. "Verra well. I dinna want tae fight ye. I wull na interfere. My friend is still up in the inn room under a sleeping tea. Allow me tae gae back and watch ower her."

Searc gestured again, and two women ran toward the inn. "They wull look after Sarah. Ye need tae stay oot here. The more eyes and ears on the captive, the more we wull learn. Ye wish tae ken where the lasses hae been taken, aye?"

Meehall took a deep breath to calm his temper. It wouldn't do for him to get into it with the clan chieftain. Especially not after pulling Eoin out of a fight with Searc not a full day hence. "Verra wull. I will bide, watch, and listen."

It was a gruesome few hours with the captive groaning in pain and pleading for his life but resisting their urges to tell them where the lasses were. At long last, though, they got him to talk.

"Tahra wishes tae alter time as she pleases!"

"She goes tae a sacred grove tae perform a ritual!"

"Nay, the portal takes her elsewhere. She does yet hae tae ride tae the grove."

"At least one traveling lass will hae tae be sacrificed. Two would be better, and three would be best."

❧ 17 ❧

Shouting outside woke Sarah up, and she instantly looked around for Meehall. Knowing by instinct he wasn't here or he would be greeting her, she worried. Had he left after all? She put her arm on her bag and was reassured to feel the bracer through it. She peeked inside just to be sure, and sighed in relief. There it was.

But instead of Meehall, two young Murray women sat on the other bed, talking with each other in hushed tones. So Sarah dare not open her pack and look for the painkillers she wanted for breakfast. Maybe she could send these teens away for a few minutes, in search of food and drink.

"Ye hae me at a loss," she told them with her

friendly face. "Ye ken that I am Sarah, but I dinna ken yer names."

She wasn't really thinking about these two Murray lasses, though. Fully awake now, she was remembering how Meehall had been so tender and gentle with her. He had to have been furious when she came onto the battlefield despite their agreement —and she had heard a bit of that in his tone as he rode her here to safety— but his anger had been supplanted by tenderness and ... dare she think it? Love.

No, Sarah. Don't let yourself think that way. You'll get only disappointment and loneliness.

Meanwhile, she carried on a conversation with the Murray lasses, who obviously were warriors.

The taller of the two stroked back her long bronze hair and spoke first. "'Tis Muireall (MOORyul) I'm called, and this is Eimhir (AEveer)."

Black-haired Eimhir had a mischievous look in her green eyes. "We heard it telt that Meehall rescued ye from the battlefield and carried ye all the way up here tae safety instead o' going back tae the battle himself."

Muireall chimed in. "I'm thinking ye went ontae the battlefield just tae give him the chance tae rescue ye. Dae I hae the right o' it?"

A knock on the door saved Sarah from having to answer.

"Sarah?" It was Meehall's voice.

Muireall got up, pulling her friend after her, and then bent to whisper to Sarah, "We wull be leaving ye tae a bit o' privacy with yer man, eh?"

Both girls winked at Sarah and rushed out of the room, letting Meehall in.

As soon as their backs were to her, Sarah dove into her bag, found the painkillers, and dry swallowed two.

Meehall just stood there solemnly for a moment.

She knew the news was bad when his eyes finally met hers, and she felt the tears come to her eyes. "Oh no!"

He held up a hand to negate her assumption that her friends were dead, but the stricken look on his face didn't change. "Nadia and Ellie are tae be sacrificed in a druid ritual. We are leaving nae tae stop it. Ye wull be safe here." He turned to leave without her.

"I'm coming with you Meehall," Sarah exclaimed as she struggled to get out of bed, her arm flaring again with pain and not wishing to cooperate and help her. She willed the painkillers to take effect, but she knew it would take nearly an hour.

Meehall rushed over to the bed, sat, and gently held her down until she relaxed and lay still. "Ye need tae stay here. Rest and heal, Sarah."

Their faces were inches apart, and there was no mistake about it. She saw a deep concern for her in his eyes, along with a desperate yearning.

When she didn't agree to stay, he went on. "Stunned me, it did, that ye would dive intae battle after me. Ye dinna even like tae fight." He continued to gaze deep into her eyes, as if willing her to tell him she dove into the battle because she wanted to have his back. She could almost hear him say it, the wish was so prominent in his features.

Without meaning to, she said what was on her mind. "I want us tae dae everything together from nae on. I dinna want tae be away from ye." The rational part of her brain regretted it as soon as she had said it. But her heart rejoiced that at last, she had made her confession and it was all up to him, now.

His hopeful eyes searched hers with a question in them: was she saying what it sounded like?

She gave him the slightest smile of encouragement and raised her lips a millimeter closer to his.

As if irresistibly drawn by her raised lips, he drifted closer and closer to her. "Aw, Sarah. I wull na ever forget Cairstine, but ye were my first love, and ye wull always be my love."

Their kiss was tender and sweet but filled with the promise of withheld passion that could wait.

Meehall caressed her hair, holding himself back carefully so as not to cause her any pain. And then he sighed deeply and got up again. "We hae much tae speak o', but 'twill hae tae bide till return with Nadia and Ellie. I must gae nae and ride fast tae save them. It makes sense nae, ye ken, what Deoord returned and telt us aboot the sacred groves na sprouting near the portals."

"Wait," she told him, struggling to get up and forcing herself to work through the pain in her arm.

"Nay," he told her with deep concern in his eyes. "Nay, ye canna come along this time. 'Tis doubly dangerous with yer injury. I wull see that yer friends make it haime, I promise ye. Rest, my love. Rest."

"I canna," she told him earnestly. "I must come along."

"Nay, Sarah. If anything happened tae ye—"

"I saw her, Meehall. I was the ainly one who saw her. I must come along. Ainly I can see her!"

It was clear in his eyes now that he thought her pain and anxiety about her friends was driving her mad. "Saw who? What are ye on aboot? Let the warriors handle—"

She had to ease his fear for her sanity as fast as possible, so she cut him off. "I saw the druid child, Meehall. She was standing on the battlefield in the middle with everyone, chanting a magic spell. 'Twas ainly I could see her. I took her doon, but yer news is the proof she's back up again, and able tae work her evil. I need tae tell ye where she is sae ye can destroy her. I wull stay behind ye, I promise, but I must come along, ye ken?"

Meehall helped Sarah get up and straighten her clothes and put the backpack on, and then he was helping her down the stairs.

They were outside now, and Sarah looked around for their horses amid the flurry of warriors rushing to and fro with supplies, preparing to ride to battle.

Meehall had ahold of her arm and steered her toward a clump of tethered horses, speaking a bit too loudly for her comfort, amid everyone who could hear. "Aye, I dae see. But ye must stay behind me, ye hear? Nay rushing intae the battle this time. Whyever did ye dae it, anyhow?"

And there it was.

"I didna wish tae tell ye this part," she said as low as she could with him still able to hear her over the din, "but the druid child must hae spelled me tae come near her. She must hae beckoned me."

❈ 18 ❈

Meehall froze just outside the clump of tethered horses in Murray camp with Sarah on his arm. The druid child had spelled her to come near? He would take Sarah back up to the room. No amount of her being able to see the druid child was worth her being drawn into battle again. When the captive Cameron had said three unmarried sacrifices would be best, he had meant Sarah should be one of them!

An ache returned to Meehall's heart, that terrible ache he had felt when he realized he had to leave Sarah all those years ago, a few months before his 18th birthday. He hadn't had time to prepare his heart for the ache, not now, nor then.

🫖

MEEHALL AND HIS TWIN, GABRIEL, SAT ON THE floor in Grand-Da Dall's small trailer living room. On the couch facing them were Grand-Da Dall and Grand-Mither Emily (their step grandmother), Vange (their mother), and Peadar (their da). On the floor with them, all sitting criss cross, were their brothers, Eoin and Jeffrey, and their two uncles who lived in this time, Tavish and Tomas.

It was the evening of Tavish and Tomas's 18th birthday. They were the oldest of all the boys, but only a few months older than Meehall and Gabriel.

Meehall had never seen his father look guilty before in his life, and it frightened him. "Da, what ails you?"

Wrinkles Meehall had never noticed deepened around his father's eyes, and Da's suntanned face sagged for the first time ever in Meehall's memory.

Da spoke hesitantly, as if he were choked up and about to cry. "There is some someaught we need tae tell ye lads," he said in Gaelic, the language they only used outside at the faire for show, not inside their trailer where only family —and girlfriends— ever entered.

Gabriel shared a concerned look with Meehall

before turning back toward Da and Mither, who didn't look much better than Da, though she was much prettier. "Aye, Da. Just tell us then. Dinna keep all that misery tae yerself. Share and share alike, ye ken."

Tavish gave Gabriel a brief smile of amusement at Gabriel's jest, as did Jeffrey.

But Da's tiny grin to acknowledge the joke looked more like a resigned grimace. "I will let yer Grand-Da tell ye. I had it in mind tae tell ye sooner, but I thought better o' it. Ye had wonderful childhoods, this way."

"Besides," interjected Mither, "we like Sarah, Ashley, Lauren, Jaelle, Amber, and Kelsey. If we had told ye sooner..." Her voice trailed off, but her meaning was clear. Meehall and his brothers and uncles might not have taken on girlfriends, if they had been told this big family secret sooner.

Now deeply perplexed, Meehall looked over at his uncle Tomas to see if the oldest of them all — older than Tavish by two minutes and turning 18 tomorrow— knew what was going on.

But Tomas shrugged, looking just as clueless as the rest of them.

Grand-Da Dall sighed deeply, then looked around and made eye contact with each person present, one by one, sharing his love and concern and pride in them all. "Ye wull hae many questions on what I'm aboot tae say, and I wull answer them. But right at this moment, I wull just tell ye what ye need tae ken sae ye can make a decision for yerself and what ye wull dae. Tavish and Tomas, tomorrow ye become men in the eyes o' modern society, on this yer 18th birthday. Would that I could just tell the two o' ye the secret and save the news tae tell yer nephews later. But I ken ye. I ken the love ye all hae for each other, and I ken ye would tell them, perhaps in nay sae gentle a way as I'm aboot tae tell them."

Dall looked over at Meehall and his brothers, who were all seated near their Da, Peadar, Dall's oldest son. "I wished to spare you until your own 18th birthdays. I hope that ye will na resent the time that ye wull miss, na kenning. Verra well."

As they all sat on the couch facing the boys, Grand-Da Dall put one arm around Grand-Mither Emily and the other arm around his son Peadar. "The time for hesitating is ower. I hae dreaded this day for 18 years, but here 'tis. We MacGregors hae a curse upon oor family. 'Tis a curse o' the druids' making. Aye, the verra same druids we run the faire for. Ye ken them. Ye hae talked with them yer entire lives. Here's what ye did na ken, what we kept from ye."

Grand-Da stretched his neck this way and that in a nervous way Meehall had never seen in him. "We run the fair for the druids because we hae tae. We canna say nay. Och, we hae negotiated with them and received concessions. We keep upon oor person the mode o' travel nae, and we travel when ''tis convenient tae oor modern lives nae. Oor ancestors did na hae it sae good."

He turned to Grand-Mither and smiled at her. "Betimes Emily had phone app tae travel in space as well as in time." He turned back to his sons and grandsons. "But those days are ower. She was testing that for the druids, we nae ken. Howsoever, things are better nae for the MacGregors than they hae been in any generation syne the curse. I want ye tae understand that, tae ken we did fight for ye. We could na lift the curse altogether, but we did fight for ye. We got ye the concession, o' choosing when ye time travel and carrying the means on yer person. Ye can time travel as an escape. You can use it for adventure. 'Tis na all bad. Please dinna despair."

Grand-Da then turned a weak smile on Meehall and his brothers, trying to put a good face on something that was obviously terrible.

Eoin was impatient even then, and he interrupted. "Why dae ye hae tae run the faire for the Druids? Why canna ye say nay?"

Meehall was glad his brother had cut to the chase. As the youngest among them, he was ofttimes indulged.

With everyone looking to him for an answer, Grand-Da shared a look with his wife, who nodded and smiled and caressed his face, then turned him to his sons and his grandsons.

Grand-Da looked away. "One o' oor MacGregor ancestors settled a gambling debt by promising his descendants would serve the druids. Every fourth-born son is a sworn slave once he reaches five and twenty years o' age. Tavish and Eoin, both o' ye are sworn slaves tae the Druids. But all o' ye are affected, because each o' yer fourth-born sons is also a slave."

Da, Mither, Grand-Da, and Grand-Mither all got up off the couch and walked toward the door, slowly, but with determination.

Just before they left, Grand-Da said, "We leave sae ye can talk. If ye wish advice from us, dae come oot and ask it. We are giving ye the honor o' privacy." And with that, all the current adults left the trailer, closing the door with a quiet click that was audible only because everyone was absolutely stunned into silence.

That ache. That ache that Meehall felt in his belly that day when he realized that any woman he married would be under the curse as well. Her fourth-born son and all her fourth-born grandsons would serve the druids.

Then, as now, Meehall realized how deep was the love he had for Sarah. He had made the decision then to live his druid-cursed life without her, so that she would be spared. And he was making the decision now to go deal with this druid child without her. She would live, even if he should die. She had the bracer. If he didn't come back, she could use it to go home.

Heart pounding, Meehall swung Sarah around from facing Snow and Smoke and marched her back toward the inn. Toward safety.

She turned and gave him an incredulous stare. "Meehall! I already telt ye. I hae tae gae with ye! Ainly I can see the druid child!"

Exasperated, he squeezed her to him, determined that she know love was his motivation now, just as it had been back then. "We wull find this

Tahra another way, Sarah, withoot ye in danger. I canna lose ye!"

She squeezed him back, but her voice went up. "But ye agreed we would dae all together from nae on."

"That was afore I kenned the druid child wanted ye for a sacrifice, Sarah."

"Meehall, I can sit inside a boring room back at Celtic. I came tae the wild Highlands for adventure. I kenned the risk. A mayhap shortened life filled with excitement is my choice, ower a long life o' tedium!"

Two Murray men walked in front of them to block their way to the inn .

Meehall followed their gaze.

Searc stood there with his arms crossed. The look he gave Meehall brooked no disagreement. "If the lass is the ainly one who can see the evil spell-caster, then we need the lass along, Meehall." He gestured.

One of the young Murray warriors rode up leading Snow and Smoke.

The smile Sarah gave Meehall as she climbed up on Snow's back was meant to reassure, he was fairly certain.

He rushed to help her, whispering when his

mouth was close to her ear, "Keep the bracer handy, aye? Use it if ye feel at all in danger."

"I wull," she assured him as he climbed up on Smoke and settled in.

They all rushed down the mountain. At first, the sacred grove looked like a peaceful place, a thicker bit of green in the middle of the forest.

But when they got close, they could hear screaming. The desperate fearful screaming of two women.

Framed by the lacy branches of an oak, Sarah's face was ashen when Meehall checked behind him. But she didn't rush ahead. Nay, so far, she was keeping her promise to stay behind him.

He gave her a grim smile to acknowledge her restraint as everyone split up to urge their horses between the tree trunks, over the roots, and under the branches on their relentless rush to rescue the lasses, whose screaming grew louder and beckoned them onward.

Bit by bit, the passing trees revealed the scene ahead.

The Cameron clan circled around the flat stone, on which sat red-haired Ellie and grey-eyed Nadia, tied up and screaming.

Thunder boomed overhead.

The very earth shook.

On hearing their approach, the Camerons all turned about on their horses to meet the Murrays in battle.

Sarah yelled out, "Tahra is at 3 o'clock on the edge of the stone! Get her! She has a sword in her hand though, get her! She's chanting!"

Eoin was busy fighting, as was his wife, but Meehall moved toward the spot where Sarah said the druid child lurked. Baltair and Ciaran followed him.

But Meehall couldn't get there. He couldn't even get close. Apparently, Tahra's magic was very strong. He looked up at the trees, searching for one he could climb. There. He turned to go to it.

And then three things happened at once: A rock landed at Meehall's feet, one of Baltair's sword swings got through and was parried with a loud clang by a woman in a hooded white robe, and Sarah yelled an exultant "Yes!" indicating it had been she who threw the rock.

Now able to see Tahra, Meehall signaled for Ciaran and Baltair to flank her with him.

They nodded their agreement and did so, and then the three of them ran in at once, swords raised.

Tahra turned her attention on Sarah.

The next thing Meehall knew, Sarah had been flung by invisible hands up into the very tree he had intended to climb. She didn't remain there, but fell screaming, her head lined up to hit cold hard stone.

Baltair and Ciaran kept attacking the druid child.

Meehall ran for all he was worth and caught Sarah barely in time, sick in the knowledge that one of his hands had grasped his love's wound. "I'm sae sorry, Sarah! Sae, sae sorry. Please say ye forgive me." He searched her eyes for the forgiveness he needed.

Her anguished face couldn't make any words, but she nodded her forgiveness.

He set her down gently in a bed of oak and rowan leaves. She was so beautiful, his Sarah.

Her eyes widened, and she pushed him away!

Meehall's world spun away from him, and he howled in anguish. He had only just gained his Sarah back, and she was rejecting him. What was the point of going on?

To add insult to injury, now she grunted and kicked at his leg, making him stumble to the side.

A sword whooshed over his head.

Meehall's reflexes made him duck, and on top of the stumble, it took his head right into the trunk of a rowan tree ...

Meehall's mind snapped back into reality. The druid child had spelled him! He fought off a

Cameron warrior on his way back to attacking the evil spellcaster, and for an indeterminate time, he was all hack and slash as he made his way over to help his cousins cut the druid child down.

"Canna... Keep... Fighting," Ciaran gasped before he collapsed on the ground.

A frightened and puzzled Baltair shrugged at Meehall, indicating he didn't have any idea what was going on with Ciaran. But Baltair kept hacking and slashing at Tahra.

Meehall ran to help him beat the witch down.

❧ 19 ❧

Sarah took stock of her body. She could move all her limbs. She hurt like hell, but nothing was broken, thanks to the copious pile of leaves no one raked. She at last saw her chance to help her friends.

She got the bracer out of her backpack, threaded a spare shoelace through it, and tied it to her belt, then draped her arisade over it, to hide it. She could easily put the bracer on at a moment's notice if the need should arise.

The leaves sure did crunch a lot as she crawled over to the other side of the stone slab from the sorceress. Every once in a while, Sarah peeked up over the stone and saw Nadia and Ellie's frightened screaming faces while she checked to be sure Tahra was still occupied with Baltair and Meehall. So far, so good.

When Nadia and Ellie noticed Sarah, they stopped screaming and looked hopeful.

Sarah herself screamed in their place, frantically gesturing for them to join in, lest Tahra notice their silence, see Sarah, and fling her up against another tree.

They complied, but their screams weren't as bloodcurdling as before.

Sarah climbed up on the stone slab to get close enough to do something about the ropes that bound her friends. All the while, she kept screaming herself, to show them how it should be done, and stealing glances at Tahra to make sure it wasn't time to just grab her friends and put on the bracer.

Finally, they got their screams just right.

She gave them a thumbs up.

At first, Sarah felt daunted at the idea of untying the knots —but then she remembered the small dirk integrated into the side of her backpack. She drew it and cut her friends' bonds, freeing them to crawl down behind the stone with her. Nadia hugged Sarah as Ellie hugged her from the other side. In this relative safety, they whispered and planned.

"How can we help?" Nadia's gray eyes burned

with gratitude, but also with vengeance. Horror lurked behind them as well, but not nearly so strongly, thanks be to Heaven.

"Think o' someaught we can dae tae distract her," Sarah said while looking around for ideas, "get her attention elsewhere sae Meehall can kill her and we can get away."

The wheels were turning behind Nadia's thoughtful stare into the trees as she combed her long brown hair back with her long fingers. "Druids get their power from the plants, right?"

Sarah looked up at the trees as well. "Aye."

"Hae ye the means tae start a fire?" Ellie's voice sounded hopeful, yet ready for disappointment, as always.

Sarah hugged them again. "As it happens, I hae just the thing." She dug around in her pack. "While I find it and get it ready, push all the dead leaves away from the Murray side o' this stone slab onto the Cameron side, toward Tahra."

Even as Sarah finished whispering this, Nadia and Ellie hiked their skirts up out of the way into their belts and crawled around pushing the leaves over to the Cameron side of the grove. Nadia's movements had a grace to them, as always, and her piles of leaves were regularly spaced. Ellie's movements were surprisingly violent, however. Had her meek little friend found aggression during her captivity? Good.

When they finished moving the leaves, they had cleared a six foot by ten foot rectangle. In so doing, they had created a huge raised row of oak and rowan leaves that had not been rained on for some time and were crackly and dry.

Sarah had her signal flare out. "See that white horse over there?"

Her friends looked at Snow and back.

"She's mine. Once the fire gets going, I wull walk ye tae her. Until ye are up on her back, keep a hold o' me. That way, I can get ye oot o' here if some aught happens." She gave them a glimpse of the bracer under her arisade.

"Let's just gae haime nae!" Ellie pleaded when she saw it, her freckled face looking ready to cry.

Sarah slashed out in front of herself in a 'definitely not' hand gesture. "I wull nae leave Meehall unless we hae tae. I wull get the both o' ye up on Snow."

"What aboot ye?" asked Nadia, full of concern.

"I wull ride with Meehall. Dinna fash, just let me get ye up ontae Snow."

Finally, Ellie assented, her voice a raspy whisper.

"Verra wull. And I dae thank ye for coming for us." She shuddered.

With a 'this one's for you' look at first Ellie, then Nadia, Sarah snapped the signal flare to light its blue-hot chemical flame, then tossed it into the raised row of dry leaves.

The flare was so hot that it lit the row within seconds. In no time at all, the whole floor of the grove behind Tahra was burning.

Sarah ran her friends over to Snow, helped them mount, and looked for her man.

Meehall looked stricken at first, but his face filled with relief when he saw Sarah.

She indicated where her friends sat atop Snow.

He nodded encouragement, but he didn't back down from his attack on the druid child.

Ciaran had recovered from the druid child's spell and jumped on his horse when the flames filled the grove. He rode over and offered his hand to help her up behind him.

But Sarah wouldn't leave Meehall. She looked around the forest floor for a stick she could use as a quarterstaff in order to help her man make a last stand.

But Tahra, nearly engulfed in flames, backed down. Waving her arms in the air, she yelled out,

"Camerons, tae me!" A blue door opened behind her, and during the brief time it was open, she took what Camerons were still alive and escaped, the portal closing with a pop behind her.

"We allowed her tae get away!" Eoin railed, along with a dozen angry curses.

Sarah was sure he would have tried to follow. Fortunately, though, the forest fire made fleeing the only sensible course of action. Rather than ride back up the mountain toward the inn, Searc led them toward home.

When the horses slowed to a walk again, Meehall gently nudged her side.

She looked down to see two pills in his hand.

"Take them," he urged. "Drink from the water straw sticking oot from the side o' yer pack."

"Let me guess," she said after she had swallowed them, "you spiked my tea with these. Will they make me sleep?"

"Guilty as charged," he said with a chuckle, "but nay. They wull merely numb the pain from that flight ye had, intae the tree."

"Pretty powerful stuff, and they can dae all that. What are they?"

"Eoin gets them from the druids at Celtic, sae 'tis na a certainty ye would find them elsewhere, ye ken?"

ONCE THE PILLS KICKED IN, RIDING IN FRONT OF Meehall was utterly wonderful now that they had admitted their love for one another and committed to staying together, even with the uncomfortable subject they had to discuss.

His breath whispered through her hair as he spoke. "Apparently, portals can open FROM the sacred grove, just nae TAE the sacred grove."

She moved her head the slightest, nuzzling his chin. "Aye, Tahra got away. Howsoever, we did what we came tae dae. Nadia and Ellie are safe."

"Aye, but my brother is angry. And he does hae the right o' it. This feud with the Camerons is na ower. He is thinking o' how Tahra wull keep on trying tae gain the ultimate power ower Scotland. How we had her in oor grasp and could've ended this, but we let her slip away." This was what

Meehall said, but meanwhile, all of him tenderly hugged all of her. His affection was overwhelming.

Her cup ran over. She wriggled around in the saddle, to make herself more comfortable, you understand. "And is that what ye are thinking?"

"Are ye daft?" He chuckled, a deep rumble in his throat that, at these close quarters, made her back tingle with the vibration. "I hae other plans in mind than confronting the Cameron clan."

She relaxed into his embrace, content to let Smoke's spirited walk jostle them together. "Good. And I intend tae see that all yer plans include me."

Nadia and Ellie rode nearby, thanking Ciaran and Baltair for their rescue and talking on and on about being kidnapped and almost killed and burned. But Meehall and Sarah let the young people's banter fade into the background so they could enjoy being in each other's company.

Meehall's mouth drew close to her ear. "Just sae oor understanding is clear, ye intend tae live here in 1706 with me in the Highlands, aye?"

She couldn't resist turning her head and stealing a kiss, which drew cat calls from her friends.

Meehall kissed her back for a long moment, but then he drew away, his warm blue eyes looking expectantly into hers.

She put a hand on his leg. "I telt ye true. If I wanted tae stay inside all day, I would hae remained at Celtic. I came here for the adventure and excitement, and adventure and excitement I wull hae."

He tickled her back with that tingling chuckle once more. "Ye did na come here for me, then?"

She squeezed his thigh. "If ye had asked me that a week ago, I would hae denied it. But aye. Aye, I did come tae see ye agin. I ken that nae. 'Twas in this setting we fell in love, although at the time we did na ken how fake a version o' this setting 'twas. The real Highlands put the faire tae shame, and 'tis the only waurld I want tae live in, sae lang as ye be with me."

"On that, we are in agreement."

He kissed her neck, and it was all she could do to keep from gasping out loud and disturbing the dignified propriety of the Highlands clan she would now call her family.

20

Sarah, Meehall, Nadia, and Ellie arrived at their Inverness inn room after a long ride full of questions about Ciaran and Baltair followed by disappointment that these young Highlanders wouldn't ever be in the future.

"How many days did ye pay for this room?" Sarah asked Meehall as she got ready to put the bracer on and gestured for everyone to gather close and hug her so they wouldn't get left behind.

""Tis paid for just two more days," he said, "sae if we are gaun'ae take longer than that tae get yer affairs in order before we return, I should gae doon-stairs and pay for another, what? Another week? A month?" He looked at her with kindness, but it was strained.

She looked up into his soft blue eyes. "Nay, two more days wull be enough. I canna keep ye away from Alan, Keith, and Lyle any longer than that. Besides, I hae a generous man who wull let me gae see my parents at Christmas, aye?"

They were all huddled close together in the room at the inn, and Nadia and Ellie looked on with amusement.

"Aye," Meehall told her with indulgence, yet also with gratitude.

She kissed his chin. "Anything else we should get settled afore we gae back tae Celtic University and drop these two off?"

He raised an eyebrow. "Ye wull hae tae speak with Gertrude when we get tae Celtic, ye ken."

Sarah met Ellie and Nadia's enquiring stares before she looked back at Meehall and nodded resignedly. "Aye, and I am na looking forward tae that, na one bit, but I wull na make my friends break the news tae her. I wull face her myself."

Nadia and Ellie visibly relaxed and then put their arms around Sarah.

"Let's go then."

"We're ready."

Sarah put the bracer on, and the room swam as if under water until the furnishings changed into modern versions, including the television, which was still on.

"Oops," she said, looking for the remote. "We should have turned the TV off before we left. I bet it annoyed the people in the next room. I wonder why the maid didn't turn it off?" She found the remote and aimed it at the TV screen.

Wait. Sarah took another look at the date on the TV screen next to the news announcer. She hit the guide button to bring up the menu of channels and today's date and time.

She turned and looked to see if Nadia and Ellie were picking up on this.

Their eyes and mouths were round.

Ellie said what they all were thinking. "We didn't miss more than the one day of work after all!"

They took a cab to Celtic, in which Ellie cracked joke after joke about trivial things. Sarah could tell that her friend was trying to get over the trauma of being kidnapped, so she let her cope how she did best. After they escorted Nadia and Ellie back to their dorm rooms and shared a tearful goodbye with much hugging and many promises to stay in touch when Sarah came home for Christmases, Meehall went with Sarah to Gertrude's office.

Sarah's knock was feeble.

Her boss called out from her desk in answer, just the same. "Come in, Sarah, and bring Meehall with you."

Sarah met Meehall's eyes.

He looked just as mystified as she felt.

"Maybe someone called her and told her we were here together," she whispered to him.

"Maybe." But he didn't look convinced.

Clinging tightly to Meehall's hand, Sarah went into her boss's office and sat down in one of the two chairs that faced Gertrude's large desk. Now she thought about it, why did Gertrude have a desk almost as big as Chancellor Stanley's?

The older woman was smiling at her as she made the last notes on something on her laptop, then closed it. "Can I help ye, Sarah?"

Sarah cleared her throat.

Meehall squeezed her hand below the line of the desk were Gertrude couldn't see. His touch was reassuring and comforting.

She squeezed his hand back. "I'm going to start a new life with Meehall, and that life does not include working here." Without meeting Gertrude's eyes, she rushed on, anxious to get this over with. "I'm very grateful for the opportunity that you provided me here and for all that you have taught me. Please, tell

Kelsey how grateful I am for her good word that put me here in the first place. I really hope not to appear ungrateful, I really do. But the life I'm about to start with Meehall just cannot include coming here. It would be too... Well, it would just be impossible for me to be with Meehall and yet come here to work. And so I bid you goodbye, right now, right this minute. I don't care to take anything with me that's in my dorm room. I leave it all to Nadia and Ellie. I won't need it where we're going. Really. I'm anxious to be on my way, so this is goodbye, right here and right now."

Sarah finally ran out of things she felt she ought to say and dared to glance up at Gertrude.

The older woman was smiling at her. Beaming, really. "Och, my dear. We canna have ye go off without any ceremony of yer lovely new beginning in life. We will throw a party for ye, tae give ye a proper sendoff." Gertrude started to open up her laptop again, presumably to look up when she could use one of Celtic's grand halls and to order engraved invitations, from the delighted look on her face.

Sarah's jaw dropped. What had gotten into her boss? She looked to Meehall for help.

Her man came to the rescue. "We need to be on our way day after tomorrow at the latest. The travel arrangements are all made and paid for, and I am needed back at... my place of business, urgently. So you see, there is no time for a sendoff."

Gertrude gave the two of them a matronly smile and nod, then picked up the phone and dialed, saying to them just as an aside, "O' course. We'll have the party this verra night. Ye can leave right after it. We dinna want to keep ye any longer than ye want to stay." She gave Sarah a particularly sweet smile. "You're going with the blessing o' Celtic, dear."

Sarah didn't remember much of the party afterward. Kelsey had been there, and all her friends from the office, including Nadia and Ellie. In fact, Kelsey had gone out of her way to introduce herself to Nadia and Ellie, even shaking hands with them. Maybe Eoin and Meehall were wrong about Kelsey. She had given Sarah this incredibly useful backpack, and she was being nice to Sarah's friends. Kelsey had her doctorate from Celtic and was a druid. She didn't have to be nice to the clerks.

They'd all eaten cake and drank punch — and Scottish whiskey. No one had seemed at all surprised that Sarah was leaving. No one had objected one bit. It had been extremely odd, but it was done and over with, and now she was going to start her new life with Meehall.

"Almost there," he said calmly on their way back to Stanley's office to use the bracer. "Will you be wanting to call your mother?"

Sarah jumped, then got out her phone and pressed her mother's contact, putting the phone to her ear and looking up at the gray stone ceiling of the university hallway, but only seeing the Highlands in her mind's eye. "Hi, Mom. Yeah, I know it's a bad time to call, that you're still at work. But hey, I need to tell you something. I'm leaving my job at Celtic University so that I can move in with Michael. We're going up to his place in the Highlands. It's rustic. There's no cell reception, so it will be hard to reach me, but I promise to come visit every Christmas."

"More often than we see each other now, Sarah. You sound happy. That's all a mother could ask. You're 27 years old. It's time you settled down. I'm happy for you."

Sarah disconnected and put the phone away just as they got to Stanley's office. The chancellor opened the door for them and gestured them over to the time travel spot without any fuss.

Giving him a grateful nod, she hugged Meehall close and put the bracer on.

Conveniently, it was now early morning here at

the 1706 Inverness inn, and they had quite a surprise waiting for them when they went down the stairs.

The two shopkeepers were at the inn with all the clothing Sarah, Ellie, and Nadia had ordered, insisting on being paid.

Shrugging, Sarah got out the purse Kelsey had given her and paid them the amount agreed, for her own clothes and for Nadia and Ellie's, too. She paid a little extra for the bags the shopkeepers had brought the clothes in.

Once it was all tied to the saddle on Snow's back, she and Meehall rode away. Even though the room was paid for one more night, she was anxious to get to where they would be living together out in the Highlands, and to see her new — well, hopefully someday they would be her new family. Meehall really should be with his children as much as possible. She wasn't going to impede his progress toward being back with them.

She didn't remember the way back to Murray camp all that well, but it seemed to her they left town a different way, and when they had ridden a good distance, she was sure they were on a different path. "Where are we going?" She finally asked Meehall.

"I think ye wull find it a verra pleasant surprise," was all he would tell her with a secretive smile.

Verra pleasant were the two nights they spent together under the stars on the way, and when Sarah laid eyes on their destination, surprise didn't even cover it.

"We gae tae a castle?"

"Aye, Huntingtower Castle." Meehall gave her a self-satisfied nod and grin from Smoke's back. "We wull be stationed here tae help serve the Murray's wronged leader, Laird John Murray, in his resistance against Scotland uniting with England. Ye ken, as dae I, the resistance is doomed, but we canna tell them. The work should prove interesting, meeting any number o' notable personages."

Struck speechless by the sight of the castle and the news they would be spending a lot of time there, she kept having to clamp her jaw closed as she rode Snow through the gate in the wall around the castle and into the courtyard, where a stable hand took both horses for them.

Alan, Keith, and Lyle came running out to greet them, visibly happy to see them together. Sarah cherished the small little arms hugging her and the wee little voices exulting in what they been doing for the past few days and how much they had missed their Da and how happy they were that Da was not lonely anymore.

"Are ye gaun'ae be oor new mither?" Little Lyle asked Sarah with the most serious face she'd ever seen on a child.

This put the sweetest smile on her face, and she hugged the little man tenderly, telling him, "Perhaps one day soon I wull. 'Tis up tae yer Da. He needs tae ask me, ye ken."

She turned her head to give Meehall a daring look, but she was dumbfounded at what she saw.

He was already down on one knee, face serious. "Sarah, I love ye with all my heart —after my children, o' course. Would ye dae me the extraordinary honor and joy o' becoming my wife and sharing everything I hae as long as we both shall live?"

Sarah collapsed down on her knees as well, and hugged him. "Aye. Aye, that I will."

21

Late nights here in Celtic's historical society's newspaper office were a bit creepy, but Nadia would brave it for a chance at advancement. Those chances were few and far between, and they always went to someone who had distinguished themselves —by doing extra work.

She was almost finished formatting this month's paper when the room darkened. She heard noises, and she had the distinct impression someone was watching her.

"Is someone there?" she asked, and then louder, "Who's there?"

Scared out of her mind, she stood up and put her

back against a wall with no windows, madly looking around at all the dancing shadows.

She thought she saw two kilted men in the middle of the room, amidst all the scary shadows.

Yes, she did. Hot-headed Eoin, she could do without. But the other man brought a smile and a hopeful greeting to her lips.

"Ciaran! What a pleasant surprise."

Jane Stain's books are exclusively available on Amazon.

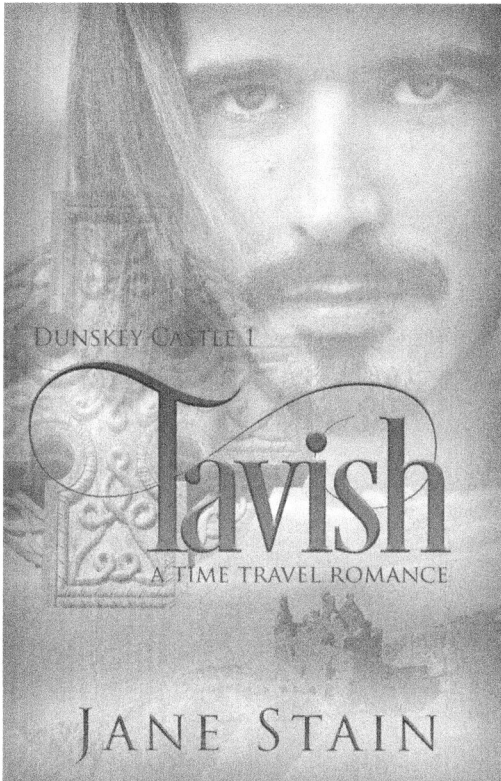

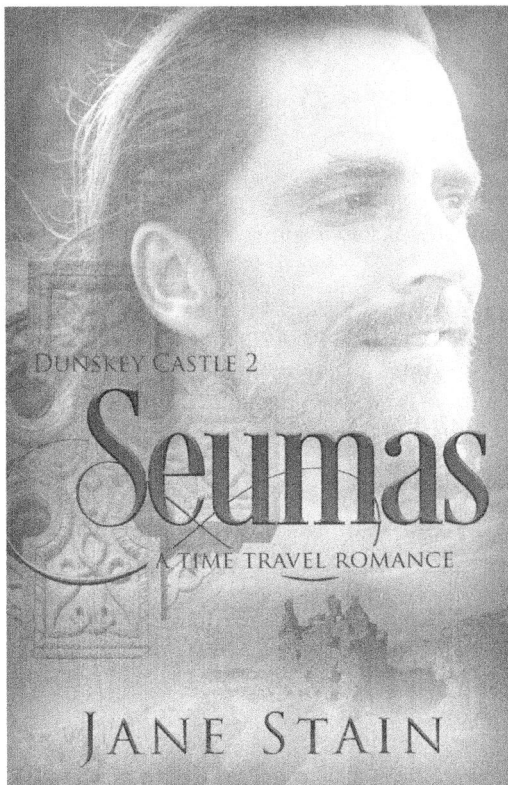

Dunskey Castle 2

Seumas

A Time Travel Romance

JANE STAIN

Djunskey Castle 3

Tomas

A Time Travel Romance

Jane Stain

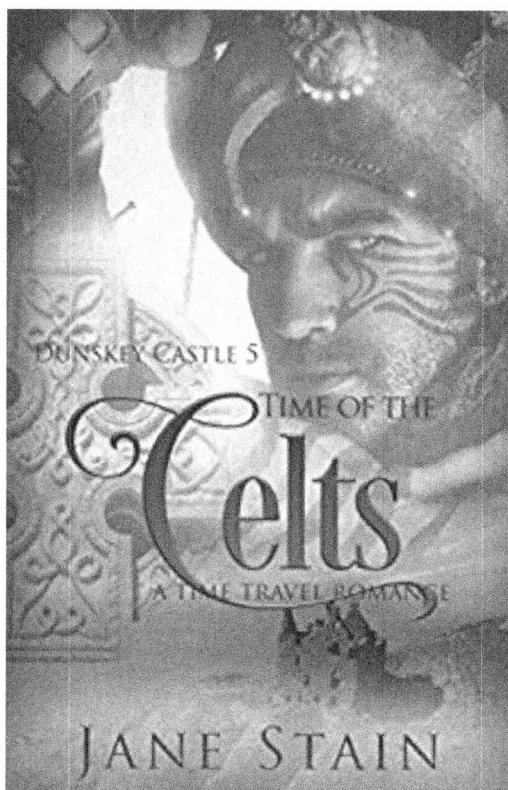

DUNSKEY CASTLE 5

TIME OF THE

Celts

A TIME TRAVEL ROMANCE

JANE STAIN

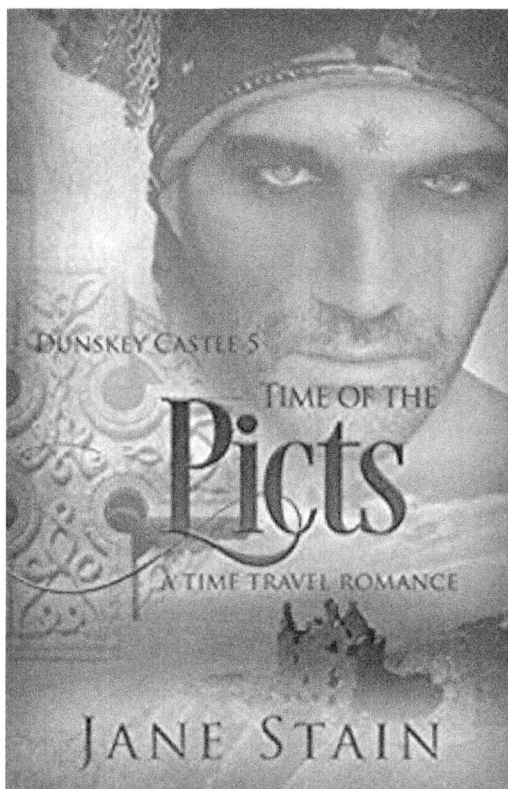

DUNSKEY CASTLE 5

TIME OF THE

Picts

A TIME TRAVEL ROMANCE

JANE STAIN

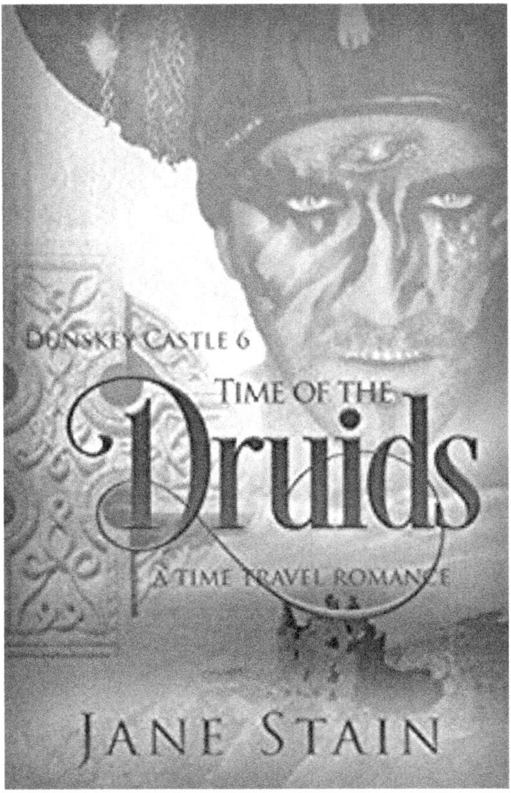
DUNSKEY CASTLE 6
TIME OF THE
Druids
A TIME TRAVEL ROMANCE
JANE STAIN

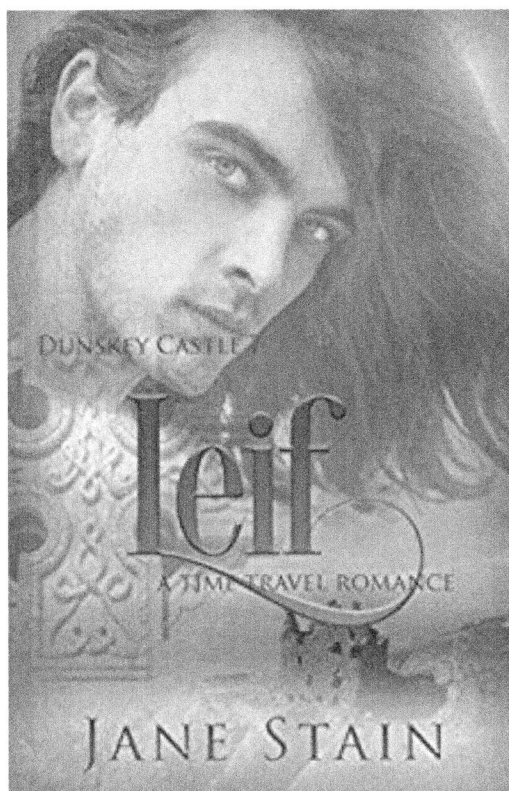

DUNSKEY CASTLE 8

Taran

A TIME TRAVEL ROMANCE

JANE STAIN

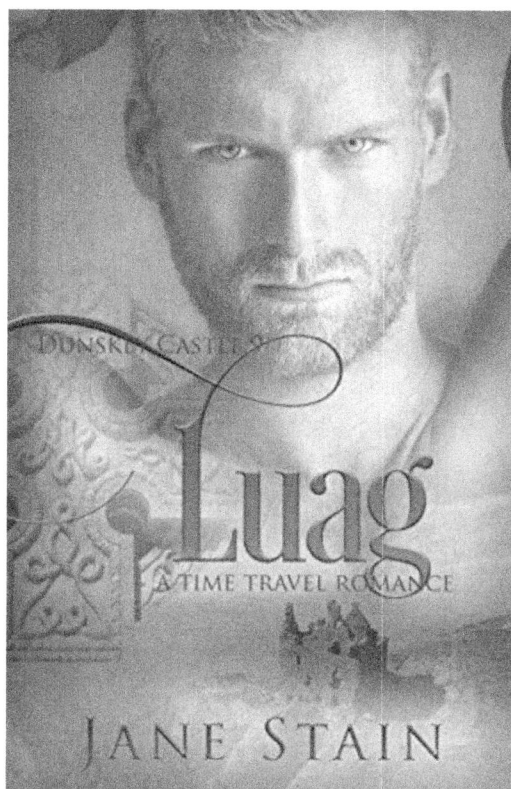

DUNSKEY CASTLE

Luag

A TIME TRAVEL ROMANCE

JANE STAIN

Made in the USA
Las Vegas, NV
02 December 2021

35888726R00132